HOUDINI'S SHADOW

HOUDINI'S SHADOW
- A NOVEL -

by LEO BRENT ROBILLARD

TURNSTONE PRESS

Houdini's Shadow
copyright © Leo Brent Robillard 2006

Turnstone Press
Artspace Building
607-100 Arthur Street
Winnipeg, MB
R3B 1H3 Canada
www.TurnstonePress.com

Turnstone Press gratefully acknowledges the assistance of the Canada Council for the Arts, the Manitoba Arts Council, the Government of Canada through the Book Publishing Industry Development Program, and the Government of Manitoba through the Department of Culture, Heritage and Tourism, Arts Branch, for our publishing activities.

Canada Council Conseil des Arts
for the Arts du Canada

MANITOBA arts COUNCIL
CONSEIL DES DU MANITOBA

Canadä

Cover design: Doowah Design
Interior design: Sharon Caseburg
Printed and bound in Canada by Friesens for Turnstone Press.

For Maija

What thing first said
"there's no way out"?; so that he'd free himself,
leap, squirm, no matter how, to chain himself again,
once more jump out of the deep alive
with all his chains singing at his feet
like the bound crowds who sigh, who sigh.

—Eli Mandel, "Houdini"

Houdini's Shadow

THE ESCAPE ARTIST

Paris, April 7, 1909.

Harry Houdini arrives at le Pont de l'Archevéche in a sleek black berlin just before three o'clock. He has alerted a number of Parisian newspaper correspondents and a handful of theatre professionals in advance of his appearance, and they are dutifully assembled at the gates of Le Morgue. Their conspicuous presence has also piqued the interest of passing citizens, and several hundred of them now line the bridge and adjacent banks of the Seine. Some of them are intrepid enough to have discovered the purpose behind this impromptu gathering, but many huddle and jostle and argue—as Parisians will—over their right to a particular patch of cobble without so much as the slightest inclination about what is to occur in the coming minutes. Or when the mystery shall unfold itself. And even among those precious few upon whose lips the name of Houdini sits like a forbidden fruit, there are some to whom the hero of American vaudeville remains a mystery—nothing more than an exotic name. They have assembled, then, not so much in anticipation as on an innate sense of the moment's *potential*. They understand that here, something might *happen*. An event they might not wish to miss. A *spectacle*. And so the throng is almost effervescent when the unassuming figure of Harry Houdini throws open the rear door of his automobile and steps into the space in the crowd opening before him like a parted sea.

The magician is accompanied by several more newspaper men and a uniformed detective from the local constabulary. Houdini is tired, but in good spirits, tipping his hat to the various women in the crowd and pumping the eager hands of the pressmen. For the last week, Ehrich Weiss—aka Harry Houdini—has been performing at the Alhambra Theatre. Two shows daily. His spectacles include a selection of phenomena, ranging from card tricks and rope games to handcuff slips and a variety of escapes—The Metamorphosis and the infamous Milk Can, among them.

A murmur rolls through the assembly of onlookers as Houdini achieves the river's edge and unceremoniously doffs his cloak, his shirt and tie, his shoes, and, finally, his pants. He is soon attired in nothing but a pair of bathing trunks—a primitive spark of milk flesh among the drab grey and olive green of the civilized crowd. The chill afternoon air of early spring raises gooseflesh on his arms and torso. The assembly has grown in the moments since his unannounced arrival, and numbers in the thousands. Each pair of eyes, like points of light, are focussed on the showman. Houdini turns to the police officer in his entourage and presents the man with his wrists. The atmosphere is one of carnival now. Buskers have assembled on the outskirts of the growing panopticon, office workers lean from nearby windows, and street vendors peddle their wares among the throng.

The police officer operates with a great deal of solemnity, cuffing the little man one wrist at a time and adding to the restraints a third impairment. About Houdini's neck he fastens an iron ring, which is joined to the handcuffs by a similar length of chain. A member of the audience is asked to test the set-up for faulty craftsmanship, but can find no sign of wrong-doing. He nods his assent, and the individual members of the assembly mimic the anonymous fellow's certainty by turning and offering the same nod to their neighbours—as though to say, "Ah, there you have it. Everything is as it should be." At which point, with the help of two companions and an ordinary stepladder, Houdini mounts one of the two pillars that guard the entrance to Le Morgue.

Houdini stares out over the muddy waters of the Seine at the crowd, which has grown silent. In his best voice, he addresses them like friends. He explains that he will now leap into the slow-moving waters of their great river. And he raises his hands above his head to further demonstrate the danger of his endeavour. But only those people immediately beneath him, who blink incredulously at his speech, hear his words. For the most part, his address is absorbed by the water and the great bowl of air above him. A latecomer on the far bank calls for the police. "*Il est fou! Arretez-le*," he cries. But he is calmed by those around him and properly chastised. "*Taisez-vous, le con.*" And then the manacled body of Harry Houdini propels itself beyond the buttresses of the Gothic bridge and disappears beneath the water's dark slick.

There is a collective exclamation from the assembly, but this is followed by silence. A minute goes by. Then two. The police officer wonders aloud to those around him what his responsibility might be should the American drown. Several bystanders step away from him. But as the third minute expires, the waters break in a flash of white foam, and the wily magician surfaces, waving the innocuous restraints above his curly head. The crowd explodes, applauding and smiling. Strangers clap each other on the back. Embrace spontaneously. They say with fists clenched, "*Un vrai artiste, quoi?*" "*Merveilleux,*" they call.

And to their delight, the man refuses aid from a nearby boat and chooses instead to swim the short distance back to the bank. A moment later, he is pulled to safety and folded into the warmth of his cloak. Cheers follow him all the way back to his berlin. And as the car retreats into the tunnel of rue de l'Archevéche, Houdini waves his departure through the vehicle's rear window. It makes a great photograph.

What the crowd cannot see is the man at the bottom of the river floating like a tethered balloon. His dark brown curls splayed and waving like a crown of thorns. His feet, buried in silt past the ankle. This man has been here before. In every river through time. He is the last temptation. The rear guard of humanity, standing firm against impending darkness. This battle is his destiny. As is its victory. But the war will forever be lost. His is the beauty of the underdog.

In the palm of his left hand, there is a skeleton key fashioned from light metal and piano wire. This is a trick he has practised countless times in the backroom of a locksmith shop in Cologne. His skill is perfect. But that means nothing here, in the half-light of a river. His pale body sluicing the lifeblood of the world. He must be better than perfect. He must race against the clock of his lungs, and he must do it blind.

Houdini has been doing this for years. He began as a contortionist for the Welsh Brothers' Circus, and eventually he worked the trapeze without a net. He spent several years touring dime museums, slipping handcuffs—eking a subsistence. And then vaudeville discovered him. Yet, each time, it is the same. Each cuff slipped. Each lock picked. Each escape is a death cheated. A long, slow look at the abyss.

The crowd above him, waiting like a held breath, can sense it, even if they cannot comprehend it. His struggle is their struggle. It always has been. They are all dying, from the moment they enter the world screaming, to the last gasp of air. He lives with this knowledge for them. It's that stoic acceptance of the void that elevates him. That makes of him a spectacle.

And so Houdini races against the possibility of death for himself. And for them. He makes temptation a ritual. And with nothing more than a homemade lock pick, he will pull himself back from the edge. He will stare down death and overcome it by mocking it. And he shall live for everyone.

This is why they cheer when he breaks the surface. Not because he has amused them with his trick. But because he lives.

THE BOXER, 1912

The aging boxer shuffles about the ring like a drugged bear. The young boy watches. The man's shoulders are curled in the telltale stance of a heavyweight. His right foot leads, the mark of a southpaw. His gloves have been cut away, but the tape remains stained with the man's own sweat. He moves with the weight of his faded robe on his back. Red satin, moth-eaten and tattered. The hood hides his face.

The crowd is gone. The managers and the cut-men have packed up and left. So has the victor. The man and the boy have outlasted them all, even the janitor. His movements are slow and deliberate now. The fight has sobered him, but his body is tired and his balance is off. He is reliving the fight, imagining what he should have done, the punches he should have thrown and the blows he should have evaded. It is always like this. A ritual the boy remembers from early childhood. It is a shadow boxing of sorts. Without the shadow. Or, at least, without its physical presence. The lights are out, but there are other kinds of shadows. Even at his young age, the boy is familiar with demons, the unseen shadows that haunt them all. And his father in particular. The boxer flails at them, ducking away from the hands that reach out to him daily. The voices that come from away.

Jake's father is a man who lives out his life in three-minute increments, punctuated by bells. He rarely raises his eyes beyond his feet, except during moments like this when he cannot help but look back.

Jake had to pour his father onto the streetcar in order to make it to the fight on time. And he had to tug the man into his gloves when they arrived. His father began drinking after Jake went to school, and he did not stop until the boy returned. He drank so much, he forgot the bout Israel had arranged for him. The first in a month. And they needed the purse. The boy and the man. But there are some things drink cannot erase. Not even shadow boxing can blot them out.

The old man is against the ropes now, and the hood has slipped from his brow. His right eye is swollen shut. But he can always see demons. The tattered robe sweeps the floor at his feet. The thick tape fattens his fingers. He is covering up. Moving. Moving. Jab, the boy thinks. Stick and roll away. But the boxer is beat. Twelve minutes. Four rounds. The bell.

Despite the fact that Jake worries about his father—about them—he finds a certain comfort in the boxing hall. He seeks solace in the man they dubbed the "Butcher"—years ago, before Jake's birth, and his battle with the demons. It is easy to love the underdog. And although he was too young to remember much about them, the ceremony reminds Jake of church services with his mother. Only here, there are fewer words and greater faith. There is a battle here, but not between good and evil. It is a championship bout against everything. And nothing. Against the encroaching darkness. Against shadow. It is the same bout they all fight, with the added benefit of spectacle. You cannot bet on evil here. Only life.

The boxer parts the ropes for himself and slips through, victorious and beaten all at once. He weaves through the jumbled mess of straight and toppled chairs. The littered bits of torn betting slips, beer bottles, and peanut shells. He wends his way slowly to the boy who waits. Who watches.

"Next time," he tells him. And then he lays a paw over the boy's shoulder and draws him in. Jake is suddenly very sleepy. The man will have to carry him home through the streets on his shoulders.

Jake sits at a rickety table in the kitchen. He is practising card tricks, sleight of hand. He is trying to remain quiet and out of his father's sight. They live in a two-room walk-up in Sainte-Anne. A cold-water flat in the heart of Montreal's industrial district. The ceilings are high, but the rooms are small. The wallpaper in the front room is peeling to reveal the rust-coloured water stains beneath. But there is a large window with a view onto the street and the Jewish grocery across the way. Now, however, the shade is down, and Jake must make do with what meagre light is collected in the kitchen window, small and slim, facing the alley. A stovepipe enters the room just above the transom, under which his father lies in the pull-out bed, and the pipe runs the length of the apartment until it disappears through the kitchen wall behind Jake. It is meant to carry heat, but even still, Jake must wear gloves with the fingertips cut out of them. Otherwise, he cannot manipulate the cards.

He has seen this done at fairs and on street corners, like a shell game. He has studied the movements carefully. Spent hours watching wealthy men be robbed of their easy money, when he should have been in school. It all comes down to illusion. Dexterity. And the art of misdirection. He knows that he is good. The school principal has already rewarded him with the strap for gambling during recess. A fate he might have escaped had he not tricked the sixth-form teacher out of his weekly wages.

His father has not been to work since the fight, and the cold box is empty. He spent his last few coins on a bottle of soothing syrup. And now he is drunk, but healing. This morning he was able to open the right eye, though it remains an indigo pool in his face. Red-rimmed and raw. Tomorrow he will report to Israel, hat in hand. His father will ask for an advance in wages, and one will be granted. Not because he deserves it, but because Israel can afford it. He will not be well enough to fight any time soon, but that is not what he does for Israel, anyway. The fights are tossed to him like bones. He doesn't often win any more. But there was a time.

Jake straightens the cards on the table. Tips up the Queen of Spades like an offering, and then sets about a routine of his own invention, shuffling and palming the cards like a professional. A crowd has gathered about the table now, but he pays no attention to them. It's just Jake and the cards and the poor lost soul on the other side of the table, hooked like a fish. When the shuffling stops, Jake begins to reel him in.

Israel Karpowicz is a small-time mobster, even by Montreal standards. But Jake is in awe of him. He accompanies his father to a warehouse in the harbour district where the criminal holds court. A freighter bound for Morocco slips through the canal, growling towards the St. Lawrence, toward the sea,

and home. Tough men lug boxes up the gangplank of a Great
Lakes schooner. The building where Israel does business is
flat and nondescript. The great doors yawn. Unlike the other
warehouses on this pier, there is little activity. The work here
takes place at night. At the top of an iron staircase on the east
side of the warehouse, a tough-looking man greets Jake's
father with a nod and allows him to pass unmolested. The two
enter a booth, roughly the size of their flat. On their right, a
series of windows look out over the warehouse floor, empty
now. At the far end, behind a desk, sits Israel. Standing at his
side is the man's bodyguard with a face like a blunt hammer.
Israel receives his father with a smile.

"Well, if it isn't the Butcher of Bonsecours. Come in,
Sean." Israel waves obliquely in the direction of the straight-
backed chairs before his bureau. "This is your boy?"

"Yes, sir. This is Jake."

"More and more like his mother he gets everyday. Thank
God for small mercies."

The two men laugh and Sean ruffles the hair on the boy's
head.

"Sorry I could not make the fight, Sean. But Benji tells me
it was not so good for you. Am I right?" Israel looks to his
bodyguard.

"The bum could barely stand," Benji replies, staring only at
Jake's father. "Why do you bother with him?"

"Please. Excuse him, Sean. Benji was kicked by a horse
when he was young."

Jake does his best not to laugh. He can see the impression
of the bodyguard's gun beneath the lapel of his serge suit
jacket. Israel winks at the boy and his smile reveals a small
gold tooth in his upper denture. He is young and fresh. A

confident, self-made man. He extends a bowl of pistachio nuts across the table to Jake. The hand on the glass dish is soft and manicured. There are rings on every finger. It smells faintly of soap, and something else. Flowers, perhaps.

"Go on, *boychick*. These you will like."

Jake dips his dirty hand into the bowl and retrieves a single shell.

Israel addresses his father again. "Now, you have come for money. Am I right?" The tone is perfunctory, but not unhappy. "Of course I am right. Benji, give the man some money."

"Why not just give him a bottle? It will save him the walk."

Israel slaps Benji's arm with the back of his hand and says something in a language Jake cannot understand. He can sense his father's irritation. See the white knuckles on his hands.

"Now. Where were we. Ah, yes. Money." Israel looks at Jake, who has just negotiated the tricky shell of the nut and placed it on his tongue. "You ever been to New York?"

Jake shakes his head. Guilty, almost, to be savouring the salty delicacy.

"You have never been to Coney Island? Let me tell you, *boyo*, this you must go see. I will tell you what is what. I am going to send your father to pick up something for me. Something very important. Because your father is a good man. And I trust him. But I am going to make sure this lug takes you to Coney Island. I will give him the money myself. Consider this a family vacation. What does your father think about this?"

Israel looks to Sean, as does Jake. He looks suddenly old, though he cannot be much beyond Israel. His clothes are stained and dirty. His hands are thick with latent arthritis. The fingernails cracked and chipped, folded about his cap. And from his face, Jake realizes that you might guess him a fisherman or some other victim of harsh weather and wind.

"Anything you say, Mr. Karpowicz."

"Anything I say. Your father is a good man, *boyo*. Remember this."

Benji chuckles.

The train takes them south out of Montreal for the first time in his life. It passes scrapyards and the tenements of Point Ste. Clair on its way to the river. Laundry floats like sheets of paper against the gunmetal blues and greys of the peeling landscape. His father is lulled by the rocking. Asleep before they hit the bridge. Jake cradles a half-eaten pretzel in his hands. He is in love with the salty delicacy, the greased brilliance of it on his fingers. Afraid, almost, to finish it.

They share a car with a man and a woman. The man wears a brown bowler cap. He feigns disinterest and boredom, but he can't keep his eyes off the younger woman. She reminds Jake of the women who inhabit the doorways of Ste. Catherine and Park. Rouged and scented. Jake stares at them both, bold-faced and curious, as though they are there for his entertainment. He is practically drunk on the tension and excitement.

But when the locomotive hits the tunnel of the Victoria Bridge, the car goes black. The sound of the train's passage is amplified and echoed. And for a moment, Jake is frightened. Tempted to grab the sleeve of his father's coat, or bolt from the car completely. Instead, he sits. Hands tight on the pretzel. Paralyzed in the dark rushing vacuum.

At one point—about midway through the tunnel—he imagines movement across the cabin. From the man. The woman. He isn't sure. But when the light crashes through the windows on the other side of the tunnel, they are where he left them. Only something is different. A smudge of blush, perhaps. A loose lock of hair. And suddenly he understands something important about the dark.

Jake and his father eat fried potatoes in Battery Park, near the Aquarium. New York's East River rolls out to the sea before them. They are there to see a man named Harry Houdini. His father says that he is a famous magician, and Jake thinks that he will perhaps see a new card trick. However, he cannot understand how a crowd this size will see anything. The boardwalk is jammed with people from all walks of life. Men in three-piece suits, gold watch fobs, and spats. Dock workers with slick, uncut hair and their shirt-sleeves rolled. And powdered women, the like of which he has never seen before. It is July and the air thick and warm. A tug sounds in the harbour.

When the little man arrives, he is dressed in a pair of swimming trunks. His hair is pushed back from his forehead, but it explodes in a mass of tight curls around his ears, not unlike a clown, Jake thinks. His father hoists the boy onto his shoulders so that he can have a better look at the spectacle unfolding on the dock. Although he can hear very little over the din of the crowd and the pop of camera flashes, he can observe the proceedings quite well.

Two men set about handcuffing the magician with heavy irons, and then proceed to enslave the man's ankles in the same way. If this weren't enough, they join the two irons together with a length of chain that is too short for the job and causes the performer to stoop. Several members of the audience are asked to inspect the work of his handlers, but no one can find fault with the manacles. It then occurs to Jake for the first time— they are going to throw him in the river. It hardly seems possible. And yet, he is sure this is what they intend to do. They are going to drown him.

"Sweet Jesus," he hears his father exhale.

But the worst, and the best, is about to come. The same handlers, accompanied by several other men in the audience, unload a packing crate from the back of a nearby truck and transport the cell to where Houdini now stands, stooped and strained under the weight of the cuffs. The top of the crate is opened and it takes four men to lift the magician into it. When the crate is closed, the two handlers hammer it shut, sparing no amount of nails.

"It's a coffin they've made for him," says a woman pressed close to Jake's father.

And then, the entire box is girded in metal belts, chains, and padlocks weighing several hundred pounds on their own. A crane from a docked ship is required to lift and then lower the box. Slowly, and yet all too quickly, the crate is submerged in the river. The crate bobs a moment, buoyed by the air inside, and a man reaches out to remove the crane's hook. In a matter of seconds the box is gone, sinking into the inky depths of the tidewaters.

Jake attempts to hold his breath as the magician must no doubt do, but his lungs begin to burn and scream for air at the turn of the first minute. He holds out another ten seconds, but he is afraid to pass out and miss Houdini's return to the surface. For he must return. It can be no other way. He has forgotten all about the crowd now. Houdini and Jake are all that exist, and a mental line connects the two. He imagines the man twisting like a fish and sinking into shadow. How long has it been? Two minutes? Three? And then he realizes that the time no longer seems to matter. It isn't about time. It's about witnessing the struggle, the same struggle his father undergoes in the ring, late at night when he is alone with his demons. But somehow, this lone man sinking in a box represents that battle on a different level.

He is a sacrifice of sorts. And as much as Jake wishes to see the little man break through the dark waters, he isn't sure that success is necessary, so much as the possibility of success. The fine line between tragedy and pathos.

And then it happens. The flattened curls of the magician's head present themselves above the lapping waves, and he lifts his free hands for the crowd to see. Stretched out from his shoulders, their pale white flame is a small sign of victory. A flag flapping.

Jake cannot help but dream about the man in the box. New York recedes from his memory like a shed skin. But the river remains. And in that river is the man. Sometimes the man is the river. Or the river is the man. He is not sure it matters which. But he is sure they are part of a mysterious relationship. It is a concept he struggles with daily. His mother has been gone for years, and yet he hopes she pushed against the darkness in the way Houdini did that day in the East River. He would like to believe that she did. He can see that his father is making the attempt, but he is tiring. What would it mean, if he could no longer crawl into the ring, or get back up after the last bell? The struggle is the thing. He is sure of it.

The image of the magician cannot be wrong. He wants to say this to his father, but he isn't sure of the words. If he could just pass on the dream, then he is convinced the boxer would understand. This is the world we live in, and we will leave it soon enough. But if you can't face that fact, each day, then you are already gone. Death must be a pebble in your shoe, a constant reminder.

Jake looks up at his father. The man is breathing heavily, leaning in the doorway, as though he has run a long distance. There is a bag in his hand. He has not taken a drink since before New York, but Jake is suspicious.

"Israel has me a fight," Sean manages to say with a smile. "A real fight."

His father explains that local favourite Avery "Stump" Wilson broke his hand in a bar fight over the weekend. He had been slated to go ten rounds with the American boxer, Oliver Jeffries. Jeffries is a young contender, still wet but impressive. He won a fifteen-round decision against the former heavyweight champion, Tommy Burns, in Burns' home town of Hanover, Ontario, the year before. And rumour has it that the current champion, Jack Johnson, is prepared to award a fight to the winner of the Wilson-Jeffries bout. Israel pulled a few strings and arranged for Jake's father to take Wilson's place. The fight is only a week off and most other boxers won't touch it. But the Butcher of Bonsecours has nowhere to go but up.

"So, naturally, I agreed," he tells Jake. "This is my big break."

As an afterthought, he tosses the bag to his son, and Jake looks inside. It is a book. *The Unmasking of Robert-Houdin.*

"I found it in a stall at the market," he calls from the kitchen. "I hope you like it."

Although his father talks on about the upcoming fight, Jake hears nothing. In the room, he sees only the book. The torn face of Harry Houdini stares at him with all-knowing eyes.

They move through the pre-dawn streets of Montreal like pale ghosts, slowly making their way to the St. Lawrence and the harbour. They follow the Lachine Canal through the Lower Terrace and the maze of Sainte-Anne. A place the Irish call Fall River. Not unlike the mess of Griffintown to the north or Montreal's other saintly precincts to the southwest. Gabriel. Cunegunde and Henri. All of them like vistas of gloom from the water. A vista shattered when they hit rue des Commissaires. Jake's father likes this area of the city best. Stretching for miles along the water. Although they have not jogged here in months, they weave along the high-level piers and wharves, past the harbour terminal railway, as though it were a daily ritual. A system with almost sixty miles of track. The cranes appear like prehistoric birds sifting the shoreline for food. Already their long necks swing with activity. And Jake cannot believe, as always, that there is a world that begins this early in the morning. The sleep is still encrusted in the corners of his own eyes as he trips along beside his father, determined to keep up and elated with the man's new-found energy. Ominous grain elevators loom out of the metamorphic sky like foreboding mediaeval fortresses. And beneath them, row upon row of cold-storage plants, warehouses, and oil-storage tanks clutter the sightlines. Below them, to their right, lie the yards of the Upper Canada Wood Merchant stacked with booms of logs and timber freshly milled in the Ottawa Valley. Olgivie's flour mill. Redpath sugar. And, to the left, Bonsecours Market, rising out of the commercial scar of Lachine like a Greek temple capped in a massive dome, replete with Doric columns. A pretentious gem. Several merchants have already begun to prop their wares against its slick exterior.

Jake is lulled by the sound of their own footfalls, clean as a metronome. He is happy. Perhaps this time will be different, he thinks. Maybe his father understood the significance of Houdini's escape as he had. He has, after all, bought Jake the book. Did he go looking for such a thing? Does it matter? His father is pushing now. The demons are at bay. The scars from his last fight have all disappeared, and when Jake looks up at the boxer beside him, he sees a new man. And, he thinks, this must mean something.

They are jogging through the heart of the city here. The place where the world passes through, stops, and rolls on like the river.

The book is a beautiful thing. Jake has never owned one before. And although he has used the textbooks lent to him by the school, they are not the same. This book belongs to him, and he reads it greedily. He runs his fingers over the words and traces the contours of its photographs, its diagrams. This book offers him knowledge. Within its pages, secrets. And it does not matter that this book might have sold one million copies. Jake believes that it has been written just for him. That Houdini would want him to have it.

He keeps it beneath his pillow so that it might always be close to his dreams. Sometimes, when his father is out, or looking away, he retrieves it from this hiding place, if only to touch it, to feel its solid affirmation. And when he does read it, he finds much more than what is written. Meaning beyond the words. A new truth in which he can place his faith.

This is what he wants to do, he thinks. He wants to escape. He wants to be like Harry Houdini. There are descriptions of rope tricks here. Cuff slipping is explained in detail. But these are only the beginning. Signposts on the road to something real. To escape—to tempt death—is to live. Is to understand existence. It is to take a long look at the darkness and thumb your nose. The act of escaping is as symbolic as the host he swallowed on Sundays with his mother. Better, perhaps, because it requires greater faith.

Jake watches his father sparring in the ring. The fight is only three days away. He is switching his stance, leading with his right one moment and jabbing left the next. His balance is immaculate. Jake has never seen this before. Israel is here, standing close to the ring with Benji. They are whispering, but they are also watching.

His father holds his left arm close, uses the right to throw his partner off. He is sticking clean, quick jabs. And then he explodes, with a straight blow to the tip of the jaw, a right hook just below the left ear. Both land well. And then he switches it up again. Jabs left, cornering the other boxer on the ropes.

The other man rolls back to the centre of the ring, trying a combination of his own. But the move is a desperate defence. Jake's father blocks the first jab with his glove, and slips the next punch entirely. The other man swings at air. The opening is huge. His father ducks in close and delivers an uppercut to the mid-section. From his seat, Jake can hear the air collapsing in the man's chest.

His father steps back, feints right with a body shot, draws the man's arms down, and then delivers the haymaker. The other boxer receives the shot full on the right cheek and staggers backward before crumpling to the mat.

The few onlookers in the gym applaud. Jake bolts to the ring to see his father and meets Benji on the way. The man stops him with a tough hand.

"Don't get too excited, kid. That ain't Jeffries." The bodyguard's face is a slab of tenderized meat.

He holds Jake a moment longer, but then lets go. Israel winks at the boy as he manoeuvres past Benji to reach the ring.

"Looks like a champ in the making. Am I right?"

Jake smiles back over his shoulder and then climbs into the ring.

He steals the empty milk can off the back of a truck and rolls it into an alley. When the horse-drawn wagon recedes into the distance, Jake rolls the can back out to the street and begins the laborious trip back to his flat. The metal container is too heavy and cumbersome to carry more than a few feet at a time, and too awkward to roll, but eventually he gets it around the corner to the base of the stairs leading to his home.

Step by step, he carries the milk can up the iron staircase, resting on each landing. Finally, he heaves it through the front doorway and into the hall. He hesitates a moment, trying to decide which direction to go. Down the hallway to the toilet, or left into his own apartment. In the end he chooses his apartment. Even though filling the container from the kitchen tap will be more difficult, the apartment is closer, and someone is likely to interrupt him for use of the toilet, if he were to go there.

Prising the lid off takes time, but eventually he succeeds. Using a saucepan as a ladle, Jake takes almost fifteen minutes to fill the container to the brim. If he doesn't hurry, his father will be home before he has a chance to negotiate his escape.

He has read and reread everything the book has to say about rope tricks and water escapes. He wants this to be his first attempt in honour of the East River Escape. The original trick calls for handcuffs, but without any, Jake opts for a complicated binding called the rope cuff. When he has completed the knot to specifications and is satisfied with its strength, Jake climbs into the milk can, feet first. He has not taken into consideration displacement, and water pours over the kitchen tiles.

It would be too difficult to escape the rope cuff and dump the water outside, so Jake decides that he will clean up the mess later. Without an assistant, he is forced to cap the can himself by pulling it into place from the inside. This also means that chains cannot be placed on the outside of the can. But because he is unsure how the chains are to be unlocked, he does not worry about this oversight. Besides, this is his first escape.

Fortunately, as Israel has often commented, Jake takes after his mother. His slight frame just fits through the open mouth of the can. He holds the lid above his head and takes one last breath before immersing himself. Installing the lid proves to be as difficult as prising it open, and it takes him much longer to pull it snug than he had planned. But just when Jake thinks he will be forced to abandon the escape, the lid slides snugly into place.

The cramped space of the milk can gives Jake little room to manage the cuff. He has slipped it many times before, but the water has gorged the rope and caused it to tighten. He tries a number of different techniques to shake it, but the knot is unforgiving. He has failed, he thinks. The air in his lungs is all but wasted. In defeat, he reaches upward to push off the cap.

Its initial resistance flusters him. He strikes at it with two powerful blows. But there is no movement at all. It's the water, he thinks. It's too cold. The can's metal neck has contracted. He panics now as the burning in his lungs increases. He strikes out again and again, but his squirming only tips the can, and he strikes his head as the container makes contact with the floor, rolls to a stop against the wall.

This is not how he imagined Houdini. The calm acceptance of a possible death. Could he have been wrong about everything? He grows light-headed from the lack of oxygen, fights to keep his lips closed against the involuntary urge to breathe. He can hear something like tiny explosions in the distance. Lights flash before his eyes. And then he feels as though he might lose consciousness, just before the water flushes out onto the floor in a single mad rush, and his father's big hands pull him free from the chamber's maternal suck.

"Failure means a drowning death."

The headline drew them in, wriggling like hooked fish. It's what Houdini did best. He was a master of self-promotion. All artists have an ego, but only the most successful learn how to sell it. Come, see me cheat death for you was a promise people couldn't resist. They were sure to witness a spectacle either way the coin fell.

And each year the tricks became more elaborate. The risk of death more real, a palpable possibility. Milk cans filled with water, capped, and locked with chains. Boxes tossed in a river. Bronze coffins six feet under the earth. The Chinese Water Torture Chamber. It was impossible not to be impressed, swept up in the euphoria of life triumphant.

The magician was a bullfighter leaning in over the horns.

Jake's father does not talk to him about the incident over supper that evening. In fact, aside from several prolonged looks from the corner of his eye, he does not communicate with him at all that night. And Jake is too frightened to bring it up. To explain. He is also certain that his father does not want to hear that boxing operates on the same principle. To be subjected to the philosophies of a twelve-year-old boy.

But his father does not speak to him in the morning, either. He disappears, instead, without waking the boy for their jog. The milk can disappears from the apartment. And when Jake reaches under his pillow, later that same morning, he realizes that the stolen container is not the only thing missing from their rooms. His father has removed his only book as well.

Jake is not actually ashamed of what he's done until he is dragged to the warehouse to see Israel. He is afraid that his father told him everything and he is unable to meet the mobster's cool eyes. But to his surprise, Jake's father only shoves a newspaper into the boy's hands and asks him to read the article aloud. Benji and Israel seem amused by this.

Jake begins, but his voice falters. His father nudges him, urging him to continue.

The article is in the *Montreal Sun* and concerns tomorrow evening's fight. Someone at the gym must have read it to Sean earlier in the day. And now, like a cat with a mouse, he brings it before Israel.

> MONTREAL—Anyone who has seen the quick hands and fluid movement of the young American prizefighter, Oliver Jeffries, will surely agree that he is a future contender for the Heavyweight Championship. But that future is not now. He has, over the first two years of his professional career, scored a number of important victories, not the least of which being last year's decision against Tommy Burns. However, natural talent and finesse will only take you so far in the world of the pugilistic arts. There are two other ingredients necessary to create a champion. Strength is one, and the other is experience.
>
> Jeffries' opponent in tomorrow night's bout has both. The older Sean Sullivan, dubbed the Butcher of Bonsecours, during his bareknuckle days, was discredited as a contender in last week's Gazette. However, while his best days may be behind him, he still has what it takes to make short work of one Oliver Jeffries. Boxing fans

might want to remember that Sullivan is a full five years younger than the now retired fighter Tommy Burns, and that he has thirty-two victories and twenty-nine knockouts under his belt.

I am going to go out on a limb this time— Sullivan in eight.

The small audience is quiet as Jake reads the article, but as he reaches the last sentence, Benji begins his telltale chuckling, a strangled, choking sound.

"Well, that sounds wonderful, Sean," says Israel. But Jake notices the look of confusion glazing over his father's face. "You must be very proud of your father, young man."

"Wonder what an article like that will do to the odds," says Benji, cracking a pistachio nut between his forefinger and his thumb. Jake does not understand what is happening, but even Israel is smiling now.

"Yes, well, an authority like this does have some bearing. Am I wrong?"

Jake's father snatches the paper away from him and storms out of the room. Jake can hardly believe it. He stands transfixed.

Israel looks at him and nods sympathetically. "I'm sorry, *boyo*. You should not have been a party to that conversation. Benji, he does not know sometimes when to be quiet. Hmmm? Am I wrong?"

Jake runs out of the room in search of his father. The laughter of the two men follows him down the stairs and out the front door of the warehouse. The feeling of shame has returned. He can sense the heat of it on the back of his neck. But he is not ashamed for himself, this time. It is his father who embarrasses him. A man like Israel would never run from a room.

The day of the fight, Jake trades an old pair of his father's boxing gloves for a set of handcuffs. Jake's classmate, Liam Mitchell, has a father who is a janitor at the police station and has managed to steal his son a pair once. Jake is through with rope tricks under water. He cuts class that afternoon, along with Liam and two other friends, and the four boys walk down to the waterfront. Jake tells them he is going to cuff himself and jump in the St. Lawrence River. The other boys can't resist the possibility of danger.

Once they arrive, Jake strips down to his underwear, and the boys tease him. But their laughter stops when he holds the cuffs out to Liam and demands that he fasten them properly.

"They have to be tight," he says.

"But you're not really gonna jump into that," Liam responds, pointing to the filth of the river. The dark foam and the oil slicks.

"And you won't be able to swim with them things strapped to your hands, neither," adds another.

"That's right. I'm going to escape."

All three boys laugh at this.

"You and your 'Hoodini'. If you jump in there with these cuffs holding your hands, you'll drown," Liam spits.

But Jake holds the cuffs out to the boy and repeats his demand.

"Whatever," his friend answers. "Not even you are fool enough to jump in there with cuffs." And so he fastens as his father showed him. "Do you at least want the key?"

"No." And just like that, Jake turns and steps off the wharf.

"Bugger me," Liam shouts, and they all run off.

Jake is a sinker without a line, drifting quickly to the muddy river bottom. His small legs, thin as matchsticks, kick to slow his descent. He had not expected the water to be so deep. He knows his friends too well to believe they will be waiting for him. And none of them will jump in after. He is as he wants to be. Alone.

This time, he will not panic. He accepts death as a variable. That was his greatest error last time. Not to have stared death down. You can't truly live until you accept death.

After only a few seconds, his feet touch bottom. Just enough light filters down for him to see his hands, glowing like phosphorescent torches. He has never practised with the cuffs, of course. He only knows the theory. According to Houdini, a simple two- or three-lever lock can be picked with fashioned piano wire. And so, Jake reaches into the back of his mouth, where he has concealed the bit of bent wire, and sets about prodding the cuffs. The pressure in his ears is tremendous, but he does his best to ignore this and focus on the lock. Without the full use of his hands, it is unlikely that he will regain the surface.

His mind drifts as the oxygen in his lungs wears thin. He thinks of his mother, who is no more than an idea to him now. He thinks of his father battling demons in the ring. And he thinks, finally, that he too may have his own demons, and that he is just not able to identify them yet. Isn't that why he longs to escape?

Just then, something pops inside the cuff and the grip on his left hand springs open. He turns his attention then to the cuff on his right. He could, of course, make it to the surface even if the next cuff didn't release him. But what would the crowd think? No, he will stay until both cuffs fall away. And he continues with renewed vigour, searching for the right levers, a process made more difficult now that he must use his left hand. But somehow, he manages and the cuff springs open like its counterpart before, and he is suddenly kicking and pulling at the water with his nimble limbs, aiming for the globe of white light on the surface.

In the locker room before the fight, Jake's father is silent. The manager offers the boxer last-minute encouragement. Jake would like to tell him about the escape, but he is not sure what to say. The boy is euphoric and has been since he crested the surface of the river. His body is pure energy. But his father is somehow changed, and has been since yesterday's incident in the warehouse. Jake has been too busy with his own battles to unearth the source of his father's melancholy. He wishes, though, that he could pass on what he has done, what he has discovered about life.

Jake is too young to purchase a ticket to the fight. It has been arranged for him to watch from his father's corner, instead. He enters the arena with his father's entourage. It is like a small parade, with his father as parade master. This is the first time Jake has been inside the Westmount Arena, and he can't believe the size of it. More people have come to watch his father than were dockside in New York to see Houdini. And the boy is awed by this.

Oliver Jeffries is already in the ring when they arrive. Jake's father receives a roar of cheers from the hometown crowd as he slips under the ropes to meet him. The announcer refers to his father as the Butcher of Bonsecours, after the article in the paper. The air is electric.

In the first round, Jeffries comes out jabbing. Picking away at Jake's father. Floating, almost, with a harassing barrage of short-arm pokes. Twice his father sends in a left cross, but both times, Jeffries sees it coming like a telegram and slips away. And again, the boy is at him like a nest of hornets. He is that fast. But he is also sloppy and Jake's father lands a surprise uppercut on the end of his chin. The crowd screams as the young fighter stumbles back onto the ropes, but does not fall. His father lumbers in, leading with his right, but the other boxer has recovered and counters with a hook of his own, tagging the older man on the left ear. Jake's father shakes his head to clear the ringing, but the boy is on him immediately, landing a combination of body blows. The older boxer clinches to protect himself and slow the onslaught. The referee parts them just as the first bell sounds.

"Cover up, out there," the manager is yelling over the din. "Pick your punches."

Jake watches as his father trundles out in the second round. Jeffries leads in with his left, but his opponent deflects the jabs with his glove and blocks another stray shot with his shoulder. The boy is frustrated and attempts an ill-timed punch over the older man's defences. But, showing the same quickness he had in the sparring match, Jake's father ducks away and lands a fast two-punch to the young man's stomach, and then backs off. Jeffries is angered by his own over-zealous punching and comes after the man. But again, Jake's father wards off each of the boy's jabs and sticks one past Jeffries himself. He follows up with a feint right hook, and lands a solid left instead. Jeffries is caught entirely off guard. The older boxer is all over him with a barrage of hooks and crosses, working up and down. The boy covers and waits for the bell.

The crowd is in a frenzy now. Even Jake is yelling as his father returns to the corner.

Jake believes he can see the old man's demons retreating into shadow. He doubts that Jeffries will make it through the next round. The article now reads like a prophecy.

At the sound of the bell, Jake's father stands but does not rush. The manager screams encouragement.

"Take it to his body, Sean."

And the boxer moves out to meet the boy. He is guarded. No doubt his manager has warned him about being hasty. But it can't matter now. Jake watches his father circling. Searching for an in. And then he springs. Two quick jabs. A stick with the left, and all three land about the boy's head. Jeffries tries to cover up and the boxer moves on the body. Left uppercut. Right hook. The demons disappear into air. The boy drops his guard. Jake's father. The struggle. Everything is just right. And then it is not. His father backs off. Circling. The manager yells into the ring.

"Finish him, Sean."

The boy bounces back, moving slowly. His first jab strikes Jake's father above the left eye. An easy punch. And yet he lands two more. It is like Jake's father has fallen asleep. Jeffries feints. Throws the punch. Uppercut under his father's spread gloves. The Butcher of Bonsecours goes to the mat.

Jake is yelling. The manager is yelling. And the crowd is stunned. Jake looks out at the astonished faces and catches Israel on the near side of the ring. Benji is there also, but they are already leaving. Turning away with an oddly cold certainty. And the darkness folds in with the referee's count.

THE MAGICIAN'S APPRENTICE, 1929

The young man hangs upside down, wrapped like a larval egg, arms fettered, legs bound and sealed in chains. He is suspended from an industrial hook above a cast iron bowl of liquid metal, the seething heat of it like an inverted sun in a sky of poured concrete. Below him on the factory floor, the last bets come in. The clock starts and the cheering begins. This will be his metamorphosis.

Moments before, he was pressed close in the human stink of them—jostled and taunted by Irish and Frenchmen. Scandinavians and Jews. Syrians. Poles. Bulgarians and Blacks. The new men had been waiting for this all week, incredulous and defiant, willing to wager their earnings against the slight man's bravado. Two labourers, picked by the crowd for their size as much as anything, clasped him by the arms. Afraid, perhaps, that he might make some mad attempt to flee. Or simply because they did not know what else to do with their own hands.

A third attendant, the shift foreman, brought forth the restraints, the appearance of which hushed the mob for the briefest of instants as they craned and pushed to see the foreign artefact. The straitjacket. Even the sound of it on their thick tongues invoked visions of violent psychopaths and men whose minds bent to perversion and unwholesome acts. Caught up in the spectacle himself, the bearer raised the canvas shirt above his head and presented it to the crowd like an executioner's axe. Its long sleeves dangled reinforced leather straps like flaccid reproductive organs.

With the help of the factory labourers, he fit the jacket over the prisoner's head and proceeded to bind him. Frequently at a loss with the unfamiliar mechanisms, they begrudgingly sought the detainee's advice.

"Make it tight," he told them.

And in response, the largest of the three men—a Finn named Olie—pushed him to the ground and placed his knee in the concave bend of the man's spine. With all his strength, the attendant drew the final belt through the polished metal buckle until there was almost no give in any direction, and fastened it in the last hole.

Then the chains were brought out. There was some argument about the way they should be wrapped. A few men in the audience cried foul play. A fight broke out in the back. A pushing match erupted closer to the display, and eventually new attendants were asked to step forward, to the satisfaction of most. As a final precaution against the young man's escape, a padlock the size of a man's heart was snapped into place. The cable and hook were dragged to where he lay bound, and fit snugly into the chain about his ankles.

Slowly, two men working the system of pulleys raised him like a pendulum and swung the body out over the molten mixture that would cool into steel.

And now the performer squirms, testing the fastness of his bonds. Searching for the weak link where he will begin. The men have made few mistakes. They work hard for their wages, and are not predisposed to throwing them away on such an action. But no one is perfect. The young man shrugs, tosses his shoulder, and the first chain snakes over his chest and falls into the tub below. A distant metal hiss. The crowd reacts with glee and despair. The shouting increases. They have allowed him five minutes. It is too much, he thinks. I will be free in just over three.

When all that remains is the last chain on his ankles, the bound man goes to work on the jacket. With practised skill and force, he presses the outside elbow under the elbow of his concealed arm. Gravity aids him in this. But the same natural force is also repositioning the humours of his inverted form, so that the capillaries in his head swell and expand like helium balloons. He must move quickly.

The next step is the more difficult, made possible only through training and a strict regimen of exercise that includes extensive stretching. The factory floor is alive as the young man manages to lift the lower arm over his head, thereby freeing them both. Two minutes have elapsed. The heat from the metal below and the cost of his recent exertion have the man rolling with perspiration.

But he does not pause.

Using his teeth, he quickly unfastens the buckles binding his hands. A few of the men curse as he reaches for the restraints at his back. Through the canvas material, his fingers are able to negotiate the buckles there in short order. And then, like a snake shucking its skin, the young man shrugs the innocuous shirt wide of the molten pot and onto the floor in a heap. Three minutes and twenty-two seconds. He is free. And the crowd is stunned. They will be working off their losses for the rest of the afternoon. Inventing lies for their wives, because the truth is simply unbelievable.

Jake works out in the nude. The temperature in the boarding house is almost one hundred degrees. He lies on a mat by the bed and pulls himself forward into a sitting position, like an embryo. Ninety-seven, he counts to himself. His body is slick and gleaming in the low gaslight of the room. He looks nothing like his father. Ninety-eight. But the skinny body of his childhood has given birth to the long, lean frame of an athlete. The musculature of an acrobat. Slim shoulders and hips. Ninety-nine. The heat melts off the excess fat. At work in the steel plant, he wears layers of clothing. Bakes himself in the smelt shop. One hundred.

Jake collapses against the mat. The wrists of each hand make contact with the cool wood of the apartment floor. The shock of it travels through him like a neural synapse. A parallax. And from above, the familiar eyes of Harry Houdini stare out of the ceiling, a poster of his 1926 appearance at The Olympia. Evidence of the magician is everywhere in the room. Books litter the desk top. Old copies of *The Right Way to Do Wrong*, *Handcuff Secrets*, and, of course, *The Unmasking of Robert-Houdin*. The tome that started it all. Newer editions of *Magical Rope Tricks and Escapes* and *Houdini's Book of Magic* are there as well. On the floor, in a dog-eared pile, are several years' worth of *The Conjurer's Monthly Magazine*, including the two volumes from 1906, edited by Houdini himself. On the back of the door hangs a straitjacket.

Jake has been performing to small audiences for some time now. Mostly colleagues or bystanders in Bonsecours Market. He has come a long way from that afternoon in Montreal harbour, that day in his kitchen with the milk can. But he is still learning the trade. In the pocket of his pants there is almost twenty dollars. The money he took from the factory workers.

He will count it one last time, and then he will add it to the rest of his stake, buried behind the wainscotting in his room.

Jake makes seventy dollars a month at the factory. For this room he pays two dollars a week. His grocery bill is three dollars for the same period of time. He isn't rich, but he saves everything. Jake has been pouring over the descriptions of Houdini's mechanisms of escape. Drawing diagrams and plans. Making what he believes to be improvements on many of them. The money he takes from the small stunts, he intends to use for materials. Everything he does, everything he undertakes, is part of a master plan. A touring show of his own. Even his work at the steel factory is thought out. Giving him access to tool and die facilities. Metal and a forge. Already, he has built a number of lock picks and skeleton keys during lunch hours and breaks.

After a brief rest, Jake rolls over. Sets his hands at either side of his head. He breathes deeply and presses into the mat. One.

United States Jail, Washington, DC, January 6, 1906.

Stripped naked and paraded for the pressmen like a possible messiah, Houdini entered the prison. Among felons and men who live life dangerously. Cell number 2. South wing. Charles J. Guiteau spent a year in the same room, staring at walls—dreaming of a new beginning—when death came for him as he had come for President Garfield.

But it only took two minutes for Houdini to escape the same cell. And another two to secure his clothes. In a coup de grace *only he could imagine, the artist freed each man on the ground floor like*

pigeons from a dovecote. Each of them flapping madly behind their saviour as he strolled into the light of flashbulbs popping. The message tied to their legs was unmistakable.
Not yet. Not today.

The Butcher of Bonsecours eventually died for lack of a lung, but if not for that, he might have died a year later, for want of a liver. Jake was not there at the end to witness the ghost rasping beneath sheets in the Queen Elizabeth Hospital. But he could have foretold the eventual years earlier. His father gave himself over to drink the very night he fell to an overmatched Oliver Jefferies. He crawled into a bottle of Israel's fashioning and never surfaced. The two men never spoke about that evening. In fact, they rarely ever spoke afterward, unless it was altogether unavoidable.

They moved almost immediately following the fight. And several other times after that, in quick succession. Each new room was worse than the last—a sliding scale of dinginess and squalor. Floorboards rotted out with moisture. Walls, three-paper thin. Crumbling plaster and exposed lath. Walk-up, cold-water flats severed from light. Tenements thrown up in a flurry of industrial expansion. Sainte-Anne. Cunegunde. Griffintown, and even the French-speaking Saint-Henri. Jake was intimate with them all in the end.

The night of the Jeffries fight, his father stopped going to Israel for work. Jake remembers their final encounter in the locker room beneath Westmount Arena. The mobster's polished shoes. His pressed white shirt. And the last payout. There could be no misunderstanding what had transpired then. Jake could not meet the man's glowering eye. But not because of hatred. Jake did not assign blame, even then. It was out of shame that he lowered his head. To him, his father disappeared that night.

To his credit, though he could not see it then, his father did not touch the wad of bills he received that night. For weeks it sat on the kitchen table in plain view. Even after they were forced to move, it remained unspent and on display. That is, until there was nothing left for booze. And then one day it just disappeared. Another thing they did not talk about.

They survived because Jake quit school. Ran errands downtown, first for a druggist named Hershel and eventually for Israel. Though that would come much later.

His father tried to enlist when the war broke out, but he was turned down without a second thought. The military machine was not so desperate in 1914, and when it finally was, the Butcher was already dead. Bedridden and coughing up bits of blood and lung for more than a year prior to conscription.

And while his father was slowly consumed from the inside out, Jake found new freedom. Or, at least, a bigger cage.

Israel has moved from his warehouse on the pier to an afterhours club on rue Ste. Catherine. Jazz is his new racket. Flappers and stills on the side, and in that order. Le St. Tropez is a 365-day New Year's celebration with a Negro band. A party at the end of the civilized world. A place where criminals live and local politicians come to slum it. Money walks in the front door and slides in from a few other entrances in the rear. But no matter where it originates, it all ends up in the same place. Israel's pocket.

As far as mobsters are concerned, Israel is still small-time. Jake knows this now. But he has connections. The most famous of whom is Alvin Karpis—née Karpowicz, Israel's younger cousin, several times removed. Like Israel, Alvin started off small-time in Montreal, but, in a twist of fate, ended up pulling smash-and-grab jobs for Ma Barker in Topeka. When she discovered his predilection for violence, he became son number three after Doc and Freddie, and part of a multi-million-dollar bank-robbing ring.

Israel is still in Montreal, and Jake is part of the money from the alley. This is the young man's night life. He arrives late, after a short nap and a change of clothes. Coveralls wouldn't cut it here. He spies Israel at his usual table through the smoke that twists like mustard gas. Benji is there too, looking like a mossback turtle in the shell of his dark tuxedo. Old and wrinkled, but just as dangerous. A woman too. Special only in that she is one woman, and not two or three. Her hair is long for the current fasion, curled and fixed into loose blonde rings. She wears a white dress and a string of pearls like a gash in her throat.

Israel is dressed to match her, or perhaps it is the other way around, Jake muses. The starched white tuxedo is better than a beacon. It's a target. Benji sees Jake before he reaches the table and barks like a good watchdog. Israel looks up. Aside from a few grey hairs, the mobster hasn't aged.

"Jake, I was expecting you earlier. Am I wrong?" The greeting is a warning, but his eyes betray no malice. Jake attributes the man's good humour to his company.

"Have you met Louisa, Jake?" The woman hangs off his arm like a coat. "Of course you haven't. She's been out of town. Hollywood, Jake. You know it?"

Jake takes a seat at the table without being invited. "Yeah, I know it."

"It was just a screen test. Israel arranged it for me," Louisa adds as a footnote, tapping the mobster on the hand.

Now that he is closer to the woman, Jake changes his mind. She is different from the others. Her eyes are small blue almonds, set in a broad face, with dark eyebrows. Her mouth is long. Individually, her features are commonplace, even unattractive. But together they look intelligent, seductive. And maybe a little desperate.

"Just a screen test," says Israel. "Like those are easy to come by." He is no longer looking at Jake. Has turned his attention to the blonde.

Finally Israel says, "Benji has a package for you, Jake."

The big man reaches into the inside pocket of his jacket and withdraws an small envelope, slips it across the table toward Jake.

"What do you do, Jake?" Louisa asks as he scoops up the package. And he knows that what she means is, what do you do for Israel.

"I work with steel," he answers and places the envelope in his own pocket.

"Don't be so modest, Jake." Israel sits back into the velvet plush of the booth. "He is an artist. Am I wrong?"

"Oh?" Louisa levels her wide eyes on Jake. "What kind of art?"

"Escape, mostly."

Israel laughs. Louisa looks around the table for the joke.

"Like Houdini," Israel elaborates. "The other famous Jew."

Louisa taps him again in mock anger.

"No joke. He's a performer. Are you not, Jake?"

Jake is beginning to find the woman's eyes unsettling, as though she can see the truth through him.

Jake says, "It's getting late."

"Work. Always work with you. The truck is at the warehouse."

Jake stands to leave, but Israel turns to him again. "Have something at the bar before you go. It's on the house."

The abundance of a man who owns you, Jake thinks, and leaves.

The bar is plated in zinc and is modelled on the Parisian clubs Israel discovered after the war. Jake orders a soda. A nobody on the Left Bank scene, Israel had the St. Tropez built the moment Prohibition was rescinded, in order to satisfy his ego. It is Friday night and the room is full. Israel's table has been swallowed by the crowd, and Jake attempts to forget him, but he can't shake the woman.

He downs the drink quickly. The night stretches out before him like a bad play. Time to leave.

Jake leaves the building the way he came in. From the alley. Only this time, he is not alone. Something moves in the shadows. He has been wary of them since his father's death. Shadows. But this time, there really is something there, moving in the corner of his eye.

Jake spins to catch the intruder head on, and meets the blonde woman instead.

"Louisa?" His voice sounds like a pebble dropped in the dark pool of the alley.

"Call me Lulu. I can't stand the name Louisa." The woman steps forward with a long cigarello burning in her hand.

"What are you doing outside?"

"Can't breathe in that place. And you? You're leaving early." The statement is meant as a question, but Jake doesn't bite. She reaches a hand up to adjust the strap of her dress.

"Hot," she says. "Even out here."

Jake knows he should leave. His instincts tell him not to look back. This isn't a coincidence, he thinks. Their meeting here.

"So what do you really do, Jake?" Her smile is weak, as though she regrets this attempt at contact. "Are you really a performer?"

"Not …"

"Because I used to work in show business. The circus too. That's where I met Israel."

"In the circus?"

"No, silly. He saw me in the circus. Coney Island."

I was there once, Jake thinks. The East River Escape. Houdini.

"Anyway. I just thought we had something in common, is all."

"I'm a driver," he tells her.

"What?" Her long mouth losing its smile.

"I'm a rum-runner for Israel. That's all."

From the outside, Sainte-Scholastique prison looks like a forbidding English manor. Neoclassical symmetry, palatial windows overlooking a treed lawn, a stone home of draughty comfort and afternoon teas. But on the inside, it is a place of open cruelty. Infamous for its hanging of French patriots a century earlier.

Jake arrived there in the winter of his sixteenth year. A cocky pickpocket and a fraud gone burglar. His father was still alive then, but he would be dead by the time of his son's release. In the beginning, it was no more than a joke to him. He would embarrass the guards. Slip out of his locked cell after dark and turn up in the most outrageous places. The kitchen pantry, eating crackers and cheese. The carriage house-cum-garage. Even the warden's personal bathroom, polishing the man's shoes. But all this play stopped when they placed him in with the darker element. The perverts and the loons. Jake had grown up in the mean streets of Montreal, but this was the slug beneath the stone. And he was forced to learn a different kind of escape there.

They cut his hair and stuck him in a jailbird uniform. They bent his body on useless labour. And they kept him awake at night. Starved him on bad food, silence, and isolation. His father taught him how to box, but Sainte-Scholastique taught him how to fight. Four long years.

Jake became a man in Sainte-Scholastique. He sorted through the anger he had on the way in and channelled it into a dream. Nebulous at first, but definite after time, like the lines on a map. When he finally received his walking papers, Jake went to the only man he knew could help him. And Israel received him with open arms.

That was the boy's first mistake.

Jake tears open the envelope Benji gave him and tips it up. A short brass key slides into his waiting palm. It is dark in the warehouse. The only available light is the ambient glow of the moon seeping in through the open garage door. The truck beside him sleeps like a winter bear.

"Jake? Dat you?" A small figure leans around the door frame and then steps in from the yard. "You're very late, *merde*. I don't like to wait around 'ear in de dark, *hein*. You never know who's in de shadows." Jean-Pierre's walk is nimble and jerky like a spastic. He looks out in all directions, pirouetting once to check his tracks.

"Evening, J-P."

"You got de key?"

"Yeah, I got it."

"What we are waiting for?"

Jake unlocks the driver's side door and, once inside, leans across to unbolt the passenger's side for Jean-Pierre. The little man leaps into the seat. He has a wild look about him. Hair curling out from under his cap like stray leaves of grass. Eyes that dart off in the wrong directions.

"Smoke?"

Jake declines and inserts the key into the ignition. The bear growls to life, its headlights like a mechanical consciousness.

Jake does not take pleasure in the criminal activity he performs for Israel. It is a means to an end. But driving a truck full of illegal alcohol across the American border at night gives him a feeling of purpose. The risk makes him feel alive. Not unlike the stunt he pulled earlier in the factory.

"I 'ear you made some enemies today, *mon ami*."

"Yeah, well, they were free to bet on me, J-P. Nobody twisted any arms." Jake pilots the truck out of the warehouse and into the night, Jean-Pierre buzzing like a gnat in his ear.

"So what you do wit all dis money you win, *hein*? You got a lady?"

"I'm saving for a rainy day," Jake answers.

"Oh, yeah. You gonna be *célèbre*. How you say—famous, *hein*. Like Houdini."

These runs do not rattle Jake much. He prides himself on his control. But Jean-Pierre is a wreck. The only variable outside Jake's sphere of influence. The wrench in the works.

"Anyway. Anytime you need money, you come see J-P."

"You don't have any money, J-P."

"Not yet, maybe. But soon. Ah, *oui*. I've been working on a little something, *hein*? A few more days and I won't need dis stinking job. No more running around in de dark, *hostie*." Jean-Pierre spits out the open window.

Jake is used to his banter and is able to phase him out most of the time. But tonight he can hardly concentrate on anything. The scene with the girl in the alley keeps replaying in his head. His partner's nervousness only makes things worse. He reminds Jake of his father. Not physically, but in the way he is always hoping for the one big score. The right fight. The miracle that would raise him up out of his poverty and onto easy street. Jake wants to tell Jean-Pierre that he's not interested in fairy tales, but J-P's silence following Jake's rebuff would only be worse than his spastic commentary.

Instead, Jake gives himself over to the woman. What was she doing in the alley, really? Was it him she hoped to meet? Someone else? And what about that story of the circus? Coney Island. Whoever she was, Israel seemed to have fallen for her. Hard. On any given night, there were a number of women at his table. Jake could not have told the difference between them. Recognized them on the street. But he is sure to remember Lulu.

"Ay," Jean-Pierre snaps his fingers at the tip of Jake's nose. "You gonna miss da turnoff, *hostie*."

He brakes, and there is a clatter of bottles from the rear. Jean-Pierre curses again.

The run takes them across the Victoria Bridge and along the south shore of the St. Lawrence, through the St. Regis Reserve. Last bastion of the Mohawks. The headlights expose the mess of ragged government housing. The fluorescent eyes of a mongrel dog. The reserve spans the New York border and is unguarded.

Most of the rum trade out of Canada takes place on the Great Lakes, in an area dubbed Rum-Runners Alley. Particularly the Windsor-Detroit Crossing. Ninety docks serve up almost a million dollars in liquor a month. Guys like Rocco Perry are the big fish with cruisers and forty hired hands. But Israel has carved himself a small but lucrative piece of the pie downriver. The Canadian government leaves him pretty much to his own devices. There are bigger fish to fry elsewhere. Nonetheless, it is a dangerous route. Especially once over the border. The Feds and the state police are less predictable. Shootings occur every night on the back roads of Vermont and New York. Last year, more than a hundred Canadians were killed running booze.

"Pull in over dair." Jean-Pierre indicates a break in the trees that is used as a road. He has been quiet since they crossed over the boundary line into the United States, but he smokes one cigarette off the next. Peers into the darkness. Checks his mirror for lights.

Jake comes to a stop in a clearing and kills the engine. After a moment, he flashes the headlights twice quickly and then hesitates. A third flash. But nothing happens.

"*Sacrifice*," Jean-Pierre swears beneath his breath. "Where dey are?"

Jake holds up a hand to silence his partner. This is the moment. The segment of the show where everything falls together or bursts apart at the seams. Everywhere there are night sounds. The high-pitched hum of cicadas, the low grump of a bullfrog. And crickets. But underneath all that is something else. A rushing sound like rubbed fabric. A native mongrel barks, splitting open the night.

"They're here," Jake says.

And several dark forms materialize from the trees. Three men in caps like Jean-Pierre's. The man in the lead opens a flashlight on the vehicle. Lifts his hand in salute.

"*Hostie*. It's about time, *hein?*"

Some days, he develops a rhythm and falls in love with the work. The monotony like a song that lulls him to sleep. Only he is not asleep, but awake and using the muscles in his arms and back. He is moving and sleeping, but not thinking. And then, there are days like today, when there can be no rhythm. When the work is a mess of heat and exhaustion. When the noise of the shop won't leave his head. When he cannot help but think and dream. The demons are closest to him then, like stray sparks on his coat. And he spends the day slapping them out, one after another.

Today it is his father. A dream that began this morning. A wound that has festered since that brief hour of rest between jobs. Between selves. He sees the punch over and over. The one that divides his father from life and death. The one he never threw that night almost seventeen years ago. There are moments, thinks Jake, that define who we are. Struggles where we create and recreate the self.

There is always chance for redemption, an opportunity to push back shadow, but it becomes more difficult with each opportunity that passes you by, each chance you let slip through your fingers. His father had chances. Other fights. But he had created a self he couldn't live with, a self beyond the possibility of salvation. And he died a little more each day, until he was just a man with a bottle who wheezed away life in his bed.

Jake holds up that image of his father. A man of self-inflicted illness. A man who died a shadow of his former self, a mere wisp beneath the bedsheets, coughing up blood in a hankie. He holds it up so that light can pass through, and he can see another possibility, a life that throws open the blinds in every dark room. A life that refuses to draw shades.

Jake's dreams are interrupted by Lulu. He imagines her waiting for him everywhere. It begins on the night of the last run, when she came upon him in the alley, but it does not end there. And soon she inhabits his waking thoughts as well. He loses count of his push-ups. Misses streets on his way to work. And when he can sleep, he finds her there too, each time.

At first he is annoyed with himself, his inability to focus on the task at hand, keep his goals in sight. But eventually he grows used to her, like a limp. She usurps his dreams of drowning altogether and allows him to welcome sleep after years of learned aversion.

Before long he is inventing ways to see her, devising schemes of unexpected brushes on the street. He does not act on anything, but there is a vicarious pleasure in their imagining. A feeling lost to him, though he is unaware until it's found. So when she steps from the gloom of the alleyway behind the apartment where he lives, he is not surprised to see her. This is how he expects to meet her now. Accidentally, on purpose. It seems only right that this woman whom he saw only once, a week ago—the lover of another man—should be waiting for him to return from work in a part of the city she does not know. He does not even bother to ask Lulu how she acquired his address. Instead, he leads her up the stairs to his room. The small space where he lives.

She looks different in the daylight. Younger. And less pretentious. The long line of her mouth turns more naturally into a smile. She can blush.

There is only one chair in his apartment, so they both choose the bed. And that is how they look at each other. Heads turned as though the other has just spoken and drawn their attention away from something less important. A game of bridge, perhaps. Or a dull conversation. And yet neither of them speaks. Neither has spoken since Jake's arrival.

Lulu is wearing a summer dress the colour of her eyes. A line of buttons down the front. Take off your dress, he thinks. And, as if responding to his request, she unfastens the buttons one at a time until she is finished, leaving a white river of flesh in their place. Jake reaches for the open seam and pushes the shift off her shoulders. He has never seen a woman like this. The small breasts between the two of them.

The Houdini Picture Corporation.

Houdini rode into movie theatres on the back of a celluloid horse in 1918. The Man of Mystery. *A serial of escape. It was clear from the beginning that the man could not act. His wooden performance like a*

bad puppet show. He followed this up with a repeat performance in
The Man from Beyond, *1922. But the crowds still came, revelling
in the world's first action films. Houdini as hero. Vicarious life.*

*No one, however, was as enthralled as the artist himself. For the
first time witness to his own escape. At night he sat in a dark room,
watching with large eyes and eating corn nuts. Master of his own
ceremony. Playing it over and over. Thrilled by his own consistency.
Each time a pleasant surprise.*

*When he discovered that the projector ran backwards, this opened
up unimaginable avenues. All night long, playing it back, playing it
forth. Playing it back, playing it forth. Marvelling at the cycle of
death and rebirth.*

Later, when they have grown used to their nakedness, Lulu
asks him about Houdini. About escaping. Although it is dark,
the room still holds the afternoon heat.

"What do you want to know?" Jake has never shared this
part of his life with anyone. He is not sure he wants to share it
even now.

"Israel says you're an escape artist. That you perform
magic."

"Yes."

"Tell me about that."

Jake thinks about this without speaking. He is not sure what
she wants to hear. And then he has an idea.

"I want you to tie me to the bed."

Lulu fastens the ropes according to Jake's instructions, beginning with the left hand. Using a regular knot, she secures one end of the rope to his wrist. Then she makes a small coil not far from the first knot and pushes a loop through the coil.

"Now pull it tight," he tells her.

Houdini made his name on rope tricks and slipping cuffs. Unlike many of his escapes, they were carried out in full view of the crowd. They were primarily matters of strength and conditioning and patience. They allowed the crowd to participate in the struggle. But there are many trick knots, as well, which, when performed behind a curtain, occur so quickly as to astound. Party favours, really—and not the sort that Jake prefers. But effective and sure to win him some applause.

Lulu strings the rope around the near bedpost and then stretches the cord across the face of the headboard and repeats the same steps backwards.

Jake asks, "Are you satisfied with the knots?"

Lulu looks down at the naked stranger before her and giggles at his prostrate form.

"More than satisfied," she says, stifling further laughter.

"Now bind my feet to the other end."

When she is finished, Jake asks her to step back from the bed. She complies, growing more serious now that she expects to witness the act of escape.

"Close your eyes and count backwards from thirty."

Lulu counts aloud for Jake's benefit, standing in the middle of the room with her head buried in her hands. Upon reaching zero, she requests Jake's permission to look. But when he does not answer, she removes her hands anyway.

The bed is empty. Jake is no longer in there. And her clothes are missing.

They meet for lunch at Le Palais. It is obscenely expensive, but Lulu picks up the tab. In preparation for their outing, she even has Jake fitted for a suit. His first ever. He allows her to do this on a lark, but secretly he is pleased. Stops in front of mirrors, steals looks at himself in shop windows.

The transformation is more than physical. He is as good as a chameleon at Le Palais, adopting airs to suit his new trappings. At Lulu's suggestion, he sends back the wine. Twice. Complains about the quality of his meat. And the staff scurry to make amends. Lay blame all the way down the foodchain until the busboy is practically whipped for no apparent reason.

Jake is alarmed by his own behaviour, and yet helpless to stop himself. Lulu practically feeds off his nervous energy like a leech, and he uses her in a different way. Her body is like a weapon he wields, pushing her through doorways like a storm trooper preparing the room for his own arrival.

He has not felt so alive since his last escape. Or those midnight invasions so long ago now. He is frightened, and loving every minute of it.

Each time they make love is like an awakening of the senses for Jake. Emotions he shut down years ago flood in on the taste of Lulu's skin. The smell of her washed hair. Feelings he thought had left him, first with the death of his mother and foremost with the ruin of his father, return so that he must bite his lip.

At night while Lulu sleeps, he watches the shadows at play on her back. The leeward slope of her shoulder blade, the narrow road of her spine. The cleft of her ass. He watches her for signs of the darkness that surrounds him.

It worries him that she has done this before, and so often. It is not a jealousy. Nothing like that. He wonders instead if she can possibly feel as he does. Or are her emotions rubbed out like an addict's neural receptors? Is there room for Jake in her world, he wants to know. But he is not sure if there is even room in his for her.

And so he tries to watch her long into each night they are together. But even he must fall asleep.

Lulu drags him to a real club on a ruelle off St. Denis. A place Israel wouldn't dream of visiting. It reminds Jake of an American speakeasy, accessible only from a walk-down in the alley. He is surprised to see that it is a woman who works the door—a small-featured brunette with a bob, who eyes him suspiciously. But after a few hushed exchanges between her and Lulu, they are ushered in without ceremony or problem. At the bottom of the flight of stairs, the temperature changes. The air becomes warm and overly humid. Jazz—only just audible from the street—is thick and primal in the basement. An exotic jungle influence.

As they hit the floor, Lulu takes Jake by the hand and pulls him through a metal door toward the sound. The next room seethes with bodies pressed together in the semblance of dance. A dark, almost breathless place punctuated by support columns. Against the walls, but not entirely visible from the entrance, there are harvest tables flanked with low benches. Almost no one is sitting.

A woman in a bloke cap and jacket, several sizes too big, serves drinks behind a backlit counter. And on the makeshift stage, a Negress blows through an alto saxophone. The rest of the band is lost to him. Jake does not recognize the jazz as Lulu hauls him into the crowd. He is jostled and bumped at first, drawing a few harsh glares from the patrons as he finds his own space among them. But Lulu pulls him close in a hip-hugging dance. The smell of her drugs him immediately.

Moments later, however, the tempo bursts open into a modified Charleston, and soon everyone around him is a tangle of flying legs and arms. Jake feels lost and self-conscious among the intoxicated throng, but Lulu keeps pace with the best of them. Another woman pushes past him to reach Lulu. A tall brunette with thick, red lips. He is confused at first—the only person standing still in the room, like a piling in fast water. Then slowly, as though awakening from a dream, Jake begins to understand where they are.

The dancers. The band. The bartender and the bouncer. All of them are women. He is, as far as he can tell, the only man in the room. The dawning must be visible then, as Lulu catches his eye over the interloper's shoulder and lets out a laugh that rises maniacally above the din.

And a moment later the two of them are careening down the alleyway. Two shadows on the wall, trailing the last notes of music from an open door. The sound of Lulu's laughter is joined by his own. The tapping of her heels as they run, hand in hand. By the end of the street, they are exhausted with laughter and forced to stop at the mouth of St. Denis to catch their breath. It is ridiculous, really. Only Jake is not entirely sure why.

The first time Jake asks her about Israel, Lulu is evasive.

"He doesn't own me," she tells him.

But Jake has his questions lined up like ducks.

"Then why do you stay with him?"

"Do you know what he would do to you if he found out?"

"So you stay with him to protect me?"

"No!"

"What, then?"

"Listen, Jake. I like you a lot. We have fun together. But there are others." This last remark stings like a spark from the smelt. "You don't own me any more than he does."

"Then what are you doing here?"

"I thought you wanted me to be here, Jake."

"I do," he says, but his voice is small and weak.

Lulu tells him one afternoon without warning. And the telling is like a gift. He knows so little about her that the story she offers seems like a world. And he collects each word like a prayer.

"I met a man who wanted to throw knives at me," she begins, "so we joined the circus to be together. And it was great for a while, but you can't make a life out of thrown knives. Anyway, not as the target."

Jake wants to disagree, but he is afraid of closing the tap.

"Did you love him?

"I think so. But things were ... complicated."

"Life's complicated."

"Not like this. Besides, I met Israel, and he offered to look after my career."

"So you left the man you loved?"

"No. Not exactly. It wasn't like that."

"Then how was it?"

"Different."

"How different?" But Jake can see that he has derailed her already. Smothered her with his wanting.

"You wouldn't understand."

"Try me."

Jake follows her home one evening after work. Tracks her clear across town from her dressmaker's on St. Urbain. At first his intention is to surprise her. It is only when she does not notice him that he decides to stalk her. And, like his experience at the restaurant, days ago, he is immediately won over by the game. Slipping unnecessarily into doorways like a hired detective, watching her weave through the crowded downtown streets. She stops before a fruit vendor to finger the produce and moves on. Frequently, she is drawn to windows. Clothes and shoes, especially. And Jake notices, for the first time, that she has a habit of twisting her hair. Left hand spinning and tucking the errant locks behind her ear.

He is almost spotted on the corner of Sainte-Famille when she turns to adjust her shoe before the passing traffic. But he moves quickly in-between parked cars and continues across the street.

As he leans against a lamppost, Jake catches her on a stairwell half a block down. Already a light burns in the window of her apartment. Israel, he thinks, as he watches her disappear. And, after a while, Jake pulls himself away and begins the long walk home.

It is movies that interest her most. She wants to be a film star.

She asks him, "Have you ever seen *The Taming of the Shrew?*"

"No."

"With Mary Pickford and Douglas Fairbanks?"

"No," he says again like an apology.

"Have you ever seen a movie?"

"I saw *The Man from Beyond.*"

"Houdini?" she asks, wrinkling her nose.

And Jake nods.

They can't seem to reconcile their experiences. After a week, he is exasperated. Asks her what she can possibly want from him.

"To escape," she says. "I want to help you escape."

The lovely assistant.

Houdini's wife was part of a song-and-dance routine when he plucked her unsuspecting from a dead-end show. She helped see him through the lean years, the dime museum circuit, and the failed School of Magic. A little girl from Brooklyn, Wilhelmina Beatrice Rahner eventually broke into vaudeville with him and spent five years touring the cultural capitals of Europe. They became the team of Harry and Bessie Houdini.

A good Catholic girl and the son of an American rabbi. They turned heads. People noticed them. He was the dark soul, brooding. The brilliant performance poet. And she was the spotlight trained on him.

Jake began with pocketbooks at the age of twelve. Random collisions yielded calfskin wallets. Gold-plated billfolds with etched initials. You could tell a lot about a person by his wallet. Leather suggested a soft man who leaned toward fine things—someone cultivating a taste. A chequebook suggested power and the need to compensate for other things. But cash in full view—tucked in a clip of precious metal—those were the movers and shakers. The risk takers of the business world, just back from a corporate takeover. Someone on his way to lunch with a mistress. Billiards at the club.

Jake never kept the money, at least not directly. He stole the wallets because he could, because he passed invisible among people. Most times he turned the wallets in to different police precincts. Collected the reward if one had been offered. Walked away if one had not. One time he got his name in the paper beside John Molson, who praised Jake for his honesty and repaid him with a dime. But the publicity backfired, and the cops were on to his schemes thereafter.

That's when he became a burglar.

Jake entered the homes of wealthy industrialists the same way he entered a room, unabashedly through the front door. The houses of Westmount intrigued him more than anything. He was not a thief. Not of anything valuable, at least. From time to time he might remove a token of some interest. Like a paperweight—a city scene glassed underwater and covered in artificial snow. It was a lark at first. New York. It had sentimental value. But when he discovered the degree of their proliferation among the rich, he decided upon a collection. A philologist could not have demonstrated more zeal. It became an obsession with him. Wanting one from every state. And then it became a matter of personal irony that he could not represent Alaska. Los Angeles under snow, he thought. Why not Nome? Anchorage?

His father came across them once during a binge and swore off drink for a week, frightened that he had begun to hallucinate.

But Jake did other things, as well. Fixed himself a sandwich in the Birks' residence, for instance. Appalled at the family's lack of mayonnaise. He took an interest in the art too, although he was not surprised by their collective poor taste, given the popularity of snowy paperweights. They had a penchant for portraiture, often untitled, but for a name and dates. So he developed a talent for labelling. *Great Uncle with Bad Teeth. Ethel Fighting Constipation. Small Child with Mole.* But there were landscapes too. Not the sublime expanse of trackless Canadian forest, endless prairies. Not the extremes of western altitude. They compiled ridiculous scenes of manicured old-world gardens with ivy rampant. Images of a fox hunt they never knew.

He understood during those visits that the wealthy existed in an alternate reality, one of their own construction. Hemmed in by iron fences and stone walls topped with lions. They didn't live in the same city as the people of St. Henri and Cunegunde. Instead, they attached themselves to the side of a mountain and prayed they did not slide into the river.

Jean-Pierre is waiting in the dark mouth of the warehouse garage when Jake arrives. His body constantly in motion. He places a cigarette between his lips, retrieves it, blows smoke. Spits. The man's head turns in the direction of each imagined sound. He kicks the ground at his feet like a bored child.

"Jake? Dat you?" The Frenchman stares into the yard at Jake's approaching silhouette.

"You're early," Jake says by way of a response. "Wife throw you out?"

"Ah. Not tonight."

Jean-Pierre's wife is a source of derision between them. One day, he will be singing the woman's praises or lauding her insatiable appetite for carnal delights; the next, he will curse her for a shrew. But Jake's knowledge of the woman is only second-hand. He has never had the pleasure, in spite of Jean-Pierre's repeated invitations for dinner. However, Jake can tell from his partner's answer that he is not up to the game.

"Let's get dis over wit, *hein*."

Something is definitely bothering the little man, but Jake is too preoccupied with his own worries to press him for details. He retrieves the envelope from his jacket pocket instead and proceeds to the truck. The key was passed to him from another of Israel's seemingly inexhaustible supply of lackeys. Neither he nor Benji was at the St. Tropez this evening, so the drop was quick. He is glad of it too. Jake is not sure he could have looked the mobster in the eye. He had only just dropped Lulu at her apartment. The smell of her is still with him as he climbs into the cab.

His affair with her is already two weeks old. And now, for the first time, he is able to fit her into his plan. She had seemed to him, only a day ago, the rope with which he might find himself hanged. But now he sees her as the missing piece in his puzzle. The last element in his apprenticeship. He was uncertain about the idea when she first mentioned it, but now she has won him over. After all, every magician needs a lovely assistant.

The truck rumbles over the dirt road through St. Regis before Jake realizes Jean-Pierre has not said a word since they left the city. His body still twitches and the cigarettes follow each other like the links in a chain. But he is uncharacteristically silent on the seat beside him.

A few minutes later, Jake pilots the vehicle down the corduroy road toward the clearing, kills the engine, and flashes the predetermined signal.

"Jake?" Jean-Pierre's voice erupts like a distant gunshot. His face is pale and apologetic in the weak light of the waning moon.

"What is it?" But as soon as the words leave his mouth, Jake is certain that the familiar dark forms of their American counterparts will not be brushing through the field on their way to the drop. "J-P! What did you do?"

"I had to, Jake. You know I would never do dis. *Il faut que tu me donne pardon.*"

Jake's hand fumbles for the ignition, but Jean-Pierre reaches to restrain him.

"*Non*, Jake. *Ils vont nous tirer desus.*" He is frantic, and, rather than battle for the key, Jake pops the driver's side door and slips into the night.

"Hold it right there, son." He can just make out the dark shadow of a man standing waist-deep in the grass several paces from the vehicle. He holds a rifle on his shoulder. Several others are approaching from the rear.

"US Customs. Put your hands where we can see 'em," shouts a voice from further off.

"I am sorry, Jake," Jean-Pierre's voice calls from inside the cab. "That little something I told you about? *Ben*, it didn't work out so good. I have a wife, Jake. *Une famille, hein.*"

"You there. Step out of the truck."

Jake hears some rustling on the other side of the vehicle. One of the gunmen shoves the butt of his rifle into his stomach. Jake goes limp and falls to his knees in the grass.

"But I make a deal," Jean-Pierre yells at his assailant.

"Shut up and turn around."

Jean-Pierre continues to plead with the federal agents, but Jake is no longer listening. His mouth gapes like a fish, making absurd requests for air. The shadows are circling.

A "crooked card sharp."

Novgorod was a city for only thirty days of the year. The remainder, it spent under water, blooming like a furtive flower on the cutbanks of a Russian river. For thirty days a festival of performances. The theatres filled to capacity. Stages erected in the streets. Some people set out months earlier to arrive in time. The town was a confluence of all the dangerous elements.

Houdini arrived among the soubrettes and the chansonettos. Just another busker forced to pay one hundred dollars to see his wife on stage. Breaking all the rules. He passed among the hypnotists and the jugglers, breathing their mad dance through his pores. But none impressed him more than a drunken card sharp, pulling impossible frauds. Transparent, almost. But no one said a word. Not even Houdini. They were awed into silence by the man's nerve. The size of his balls.

Jean-Pierre would not shut up until the authorities broke his nose. Now he sits opposite Jake, propped against the metal wall of the paddy wagon. The only movement he makes is when the vehicle strikes a pothole and tosses him from side to side. Jake has never seen him so still. His face looks like a hip of raw beef. The nose repositioned in the geography of his head. His eyes are closed.

A small window separates the cab of the vehicle from the holding tank where they sit. Jake takes notice of the two guards up front. As far as he can tell, there are no other automobiles in pursuit. He guesses that the other agents will be dividing the spoils and deciding how much to turn in.

He inspects the cuffs about his wrists, common enough. Not unlike the various sets he owns for rehearsal, in fact. All he needs is a piece of wire thin enough. And then he looks to Jean-Pierre.

"Are you wearing a crucifix?" Jake asks him in his best broken French. Trying not to give anything away to their captors. The man's eyes open slowly in response. They are both slowly turning black. He stares a moment as though surfacing from a dream.

"*Pourquoi?*"

"Keep it down back there," the officer in the passenger seat bellows, tapping the bars that separate them with a club.

Jean-Pierre nods.

"*Passe-moi-la,*" Jake whispers.

The beaten man looks through the window at the guards. And then, satisfied that they are oblivious, he pulls the slim gold chain over his head and dangles it between them. Jake reaches across with both hands and snatches it away.

The little Jesus figure hangs its head in despair. Arms pinned. Long legs nailed to a cross. Jake sticks the horizontal beam into the keyhole of his left cuff and bends it so that it snaps.

"*Hein!*" Jean-Pierre whispers, berating him for the blatant iconoclasm.

Jake looks at him with cold eyes and dumps the broken arm on the floor. Jean-Pierre watches, amazed, as his partner flips the figure over and fishes around in the lock's mechanism. The speed at which he is able to dispatch either cuff is almost anti-climactic.

Jean-Pierre holds out his hands expectantly. But Jake does not move to help him. The trapped man shakes his arms instantly. Looks up into his face.

"*Je te prie,*" he begs.

And Jake acquiesces.

"But we split after we escape," he warns. "Don't follow me."

Jean-Pierre's eyes well up. He cannot be sure if it is due to the broken nose, but Jake does not care either way. When the cuffs are gelded, he turns his attention to the door. How far have they travelled? he wonders. Two, maybe three miles. He is not sure that they are still on the reservation, but the vehicle has not left the main road.

From the inside, he cannot access the lock. But when they were loaded on to the wagon, he noticed a manual lever on the outside of the rear door. Jake tosses his jacket on the floor and pulls his shirt over his head. Jean-Pierre is restless again. Looking to Jake and then back to the guards in the front seat.

"*Vas-y vite.*" A moment later he hisses, "Quickly."

Jake ties the shirtsleeves in a knot with one another, so that they form a continuous circle. This he dangles through the bars in the rear door. He cannot see from this angle. Stones and dust spit upward and out into the wagon's light motes. It takes longer than he would like, but eventually Jake catches the outstretched arm of the door's locking system. He pulls upward abruptly and the metal rod makes a grating sound like a large, rusted hinge. However, the shirt slips as the angle of the lever increases, and Jake falls backward onto the floor of the holding tank. The lock is not entirely free.

"Hey, what's going on back there?" Both officers crane to see back into the wagon. Their dark, inquisitive faces are like two cows at a fence.

From his seated position, Jake rocks onto his back and propels himself forward, lashing out with both feet. The door pops open under the pressure and bounces outward.

Jean-Pierre leaps over Jake's prostrate form into the rush of air.

"No," Jake grunts too late.

The driver stomps on the brake, sending Jake sliding to the front of the wagon. But he recovers quickly and scrambles toward the open door.

Once outside, Jake dives into the salvation of the forest. Branches and twigs tear at his exposed torso. Slap at his face. Twice he stumbles over a root before he thinks to slow down. Over the shouts of the pursuing guards, he can hear the cries of his partner, a hundred yards or more back on the road. At the speed they were travelling, Jake is sure that the man has broken a leg. Or worse. Even if he makes it off the road, he will be crippled. The guards will find him in the light or stumble across him in the dark. Either way, he is finished.

Just then, a rifle cracks open the night, and the screaming stops. Jake turns and picks his way carefully north.

Once the adrenaline has burnt off, Jake begins to discover the emerald dark of the forest. His ribs are smashed where the butt of the officer's rifle struck him. It is difficult to catch a proper breath. Above him, a thick canopy of leaves blankets the stars, making navigation a game of guesswork at best. The reality of his situation slowly creeps into his consciousness. J-P is dead, and he is a wounded man stumbling about in the night.

He wants to hold onto his dead friend's face, the mischievous wink. But already this is lost to him. In fact, he cannot keep his mind on the situation at all. Lulu reaches out to him even here. Her scent. The taste of her on his tongue. The milk white blink of skin on the underside of her wrists. She has become a danger to him, an inopportune thought. Jake has paid dearly for her memory already, and he knows that he must purge himself of her before dawn if he is to make his escape.

Jake fingers the tender flesh beneath his heart. Thinks only *hurt*. And walks the long way into morning.

The Valentine's Day Massacre made the front page of every paper in North America. Its story stood as a warning to the dangers of alcohol. And rum-runners in Canada paid heed. Jake marvelled at the brutality of it. The audacity and the simplicity of its execution. Capone at his storytelling best.

The papers recreated what must have occurred from the conditions of the crime scene and a few anonymous tips. Certain details remained hazy, but the bulk of the story was there.

Seven men in expensive suits were picked up in a routine sweep. They were "named." Big shots in the Bugs Moran liquor empire. A prentender to the Capone throne. But the sweep was anything but regular.

The men laughed at the cops' impertinence. Lit cigarettes and told jokes about the cops' mothers. But when they were lined up against the warehouse wall, two other men entered with Tommy guns. It was the line of bullet-broken bodies that made the paper. Rum-running was big business, the competition fierce. If the big shots were fair game, Jake was only incidental.

Jake arrives at a service station just as the sun appears over his right shoulder. There are several transport trucks parked in the lot like sleeping dogs. Miraculously, he has found his way through the night. He cannot be more than a few miles from the border now. Exhausted from the first leg of his odyssey, Jake surveys the area for any sign of life. But nothing stirs beyond the flicker of a few wayward sparrows.

Acting quickly, he moves across the gravel lot as quietly as possible, cradling his fractured chest like an infant. There is an apartment with a sunken porch at the back of the service station. The roof tilts at a dangerous angle. But from one of the rotting pillars, a long line of wash extends over the bare yard to a post. This is what he wants. And, to his relief, the eye hooks slip easily from their flaking beds.

The truck is not important, so Jake chooses the one closest to him. Time is at a premium. With much difficulty, he manages to slide underneath its trailer, working through the pain. He is a wonder with knots, and it takes him only a minute to rig the harness that will hold him. A moment more to secure it to the chassis.

A half-hour later, when the engine finally stutters to life, he is stuck to the vehicle like a webbed fly.

The road is paved and smooth for the most part, but the rattle of the old engine is enough to jar bones. And sometimes a stray stone is pitched up by the wheels, ricocheting off the undercarriage at a dangerous velocity. Several times Jake is hit with the missiles. Welts bloom like roses beneath his shirt and trousers. The worst is a stone that grazes his ear, taking a small chunk of the lobe away. But throughout the ordeal, his harness holds.

The border crossing is anti-climactic in comparison. The transport slows at the booth but is waved through without a second glance. It is cargo moving in the opposite direction that concerns them the most.

After this, the truck makes tracks along the same roads that carried him out of Montreal the evening before. On the corner of Sherbrooke and Pine, the trucker gears down for a traffic light. Jake is numb from the constant vibration—the lack of sleep—but he manages to slip the knots. When the truck pulls away, he remains still in its wake. The mid-morning traffic stops dumb. Pedestrians marvel at his strange birth.

Jake cannot return to his apartment. The details of J-P's confession might have included names and, if that is the case, his apartment may already be under surveillance. If they search enough, they will find the stack of cash he has been squirrelling away for years. He cannot begin to imagine the loss.

The truck ride has given him time for alternative plans, so, when he drops from the belly of the beast, Jake runs straight to Lulu.

She lives on the main floor of a three-storey stone mansard building on Sainte-Famille. An outdoor staircase leads to her entrance. It is an anonymous building among others that appear in almost identical fashion up and down the street. But the neighbourhood is several steps up from his own neighbourhood in Sainte-Anne. Her apartment is empty when he arrives at noon, but he lets himself in with the help of a penknife. It is the first time he breaches the doorway, but exhaustion wins out over curiosity and forces him to the sofa without so much as a peek. The blinds are drawn against the sun, and he remains there in a soundless slumber until early evening, when he awakens thirsty and famished.

Jake forages through the kitchen cupboards, settling on bread and cheese. His movements are slow, but he has grown used to the throb in his chest. Not broken, he thinks. But bruised. It is the headache emanating from his damaged ear that weighs most heavily upon him now. He walks through the rooms like a ghost, absorbing the character of their primary occupant. Never has he experienced the freedom of space. He eats while he moves, trailing bread crumbs over the various carpets and stretches of polished parquet. With his free hand, Jake combs over the horizontal surfaces, making tracks in the dust, like a dog leaking scent.

A photograph of Lulu hangs over the mantelpiece. She is dressed in sequins and feathers. Her arms are bound to a wheel. Knives protrude from the spokes. This he picks up and carries into the bedroom. The sheets on the oversized bed are tangled and turned down. He proceeds to the wardrobe, where, among rows of dresses, Jake finds the pressed shirts of a man. Dark suit jackets. Vests and shoes. The articles must belong to Israel, he thinks, and then contemplates leaving. But then where would he go? Instead, Jake removes his clothing and tosses the various articles carelessly over a bureau chair.

Naked, he enters the bathroom, headed for the shower. The luxury of plumbing. Hot water.

Jake's eventual capture was inevitable. His late-night raids were beginning to make the papers. They dubbed him the Sleepwalker in one column and the epithet stuck. In retrospect, he thinks that perhaps he might have yearned for that capture. His real name beside that other moniker like a badge. But it is difficult to say, really. He was confused then. But the newsmen were closer to the truth than even they imagined. Jake did not sleep. Had become an insomniac, slowly relinquishing rest. He was plagued by shadows and lonely dreams of drowning.

His body was wasted. Cavernous eyes and cheeks to match. Naked, his torso resembled a Venetian blind. The last home he entered was a Georgian manor high on the hill, not far from the belvedere. He had been on his way to the city's lookout when it called to him like a siren. The front door swung open on its hinges without need of a pick. It was as though the house had been waiting for him. The prodigal son returned.

He inhabited the rooms downstairs like a cat, brushing up against furniture as he passed. Bored, almost, after the initial rush. Jake saved the kitchen for last. Hunger arrived as an afterthought. The moon was on the other side of the house when he entered, and the room was a silent cave. But he knew immediately someone else was there. The hairs on the nape of his neck, sharp as quills.

When his eyes had adjusted to the black, he could see her like a pale moon at the table. Jake shrugged and drew up a chair. She did not move. From closer, he could sketch out the glass of milk, half empty. A white pool in front of her. The glass invisible. For several minutes they stared across the table at one another without speaking. Features appeared over time like degrees of light and shadow in a photographer's emulsion.

It was the girl who spoke first, her mouth a dark eye blinking. "Are you hungry?"

"No," he lied and regretted it immediately.

"I'll make you a sandwich," she said anyway.

"No, thank you," he persisted. "Can't sleep?"

But the girl only shook her head in response.

"Me either."

"You have nightmares," she said, but Jake was not sure if it was a question or a fact, and so he did not answer. Reached across the table for the milk, instead.

"May I?"

"I can get you a glass of your own." She was ten, perhaps a small twelve. Six years his junior. Voice like a munchkin.

"Just a sip," he said, and the girl acquiesced.

"My father wouldn't like it if he knew you were here," she said as he was swallowing the drink.

He used his sleeve to clean his mouth. "I won't tell if you won't."

The girl nodded, and Jake smiled in response, but the milk and the late hour had worked their toll on him. For the first time in months, he was physically exhausted. The girl's presence was like a warm blanket. His eyes closed.

"I'm just going to lay my head down for a few minutes," he said.

"You should leave. It will be morning soon," she answered. But Jake's head was already folded in his arms.

"Wake me," he said and drifted off.

That's how they were found the next morning. Across the table from one another, heads bowed. Sleeping peacefully.

He is standing immobile under the water's warm rush when the curtain is pulled back. A moment later, he comes to on the slick, tiled floor. Water continues to pound into the tub, splashing over the unprotected length where the curtain is missing. A young man looms above his foetal mass. The edge of a switchblade presses into his throat. Without thinking, Jake lifts his right knee into the attacker's unprotected crotch. It does not elicit the desired crippling, but it does allow Jake a chance to bat the man's hand away and roll to relative safety. The young man comes at him again, but Jake sidesteps the attempt easily and delivers a solid blow to his assailant's stomach. Air escapes in a high-pitched wheeze and the man stumbles backward into the bedroom. Jake slides over the tiles and catches himself on the door frame. The man is doubled over on his hands and knees, searching for the dropped knife. Jake steps onto the plush carpet and delivers a powerful blow to his cheek that sends him crashing into the vanity. The glass mirror breaks off in shards, falling around his attacker like the fragments of a Christmas tree ornament. Jake's breath is laboured. A sharp pain in his chest forces him to pause. But when he moves in again to finish off his assailant, Lulu's scream stops him dead in his tracks.

"Bobby! Jake, no."

Jake looks from one to the other as Lulu rushes in and cradles the young man's head in her arms. For the first time, Jake is able to examine his opponent at length as he lowers himself to the floor. He is no more than a swarthy kid with a pencil-thin moustache and feminine cheekbones. He is probably shorter than Lulu, but harder, with dark, foreboding eyes.

Jake cannot be sure, but it appears as though he is crying softly and furtively, pushing away the woman's ministering arms.

Lulu explains that Bobby has been following her around like a lovesick puppy ever since she arrived in Montreal.

"He was a medical student at the university, living off his father's trust. Or something," she explains. "But he dropped out and the purse strings have been pulled shut."

"What is he doing here?" Jake demands.

Lulu raises her finger to her lips and closes the door to her bedroom.

"You're not going to let him sleep out there?"

"He has nowhere else to go. Besides, he's harmless."

Jake flips the switchblade he collected from the floor and lays it on the remains of the vanity.

"He was protecting me, Jake."

Lulu tells him she will ask Israel to help the boy. To give him a job. And then he will be able to find a room of his own.

"Now, perhaps you could explain your presence."

Lulu's voice loses its edge as Jake relates the story of his rum-run the night before. She has him strip off his clothes so she can examine the various wounds. And slowly, quietly, they make love, so that Bobby will not hear them.

Book notes.

Houdini was a man of little formal education, a fact that bothered him later as he moved among the rich. He had learned at an early age to live by his wits, and that attitude had done well by him among jugglers, buskers, and illusionists like himself. But when he left the world of vaudeville behind, he discovered a new barometer.

He attacked reading as he pursued a new escape. His wealth purchased him the world's finest library devoted almost entirely to magic. Mahogany shelves, leather-bound first editions, and a rolling ladder to reach them. Houdini came to love books in the end. Evenings under a reading lamp in his favourite chair, he would hold them open in his lap. Pass fingers over coloured plates, spines of gold leaf.

He had become a king by then and entered a new arena. Danger was redundant.

Jake dresses in the half-light of the drawn shades. He steals one of Israel's shirts from the rack. It is small, but not overly uncomfortable. Lulu is oblivious. His ribs are stiff from the incident the night before, his hand slightly swollen from the fight. He tries not to make a sound as he slips from the bedroom to the parlour, closing the door carefully behind him. He expects to find the boy asleep in the next room, but the chesterfield is empty. A blanket lies crumpled over one arm.

It disturbs Jake to know that Bobby was moving around in the apartment while he slept unaware, but he is also pleased to know the boy is gone, that Lulu is not at risk. Jake is not at all at ease with her current living arrangements. Their relationship was complicated enough with only Israel in the way. This new obstacle has caught like a stiff left jab. He can barely consider it under the present circumstances. Israel's loss. The death of Jean-Pierre. The widow he intends to visit.

Just as the sun washes into the harbour, Jake walks into the grid of Saint-Henri. Treeless streets and yardless, wood-frame houses lean over the sidewalks. In his mind, he has only a number. A pearl dropped in his palm weeks ago, when Jean-Pierre was alive and Lulu was not even an embryonic thought. Jake has no expectations about what he will find today. He isn't even convinced that he will find anything. Jean-Pierre was a schemer—a con man and a snitch. But Jake must know for sure. He did not feel strongly enough about Jean-Pierre to ever consider whether he liked him, but surely the man deserved the courtesy of a death notice. And so Jake tramps the treeless expanse of poverty-infested slums down Esplanade in search of a possible widow. A label she wears ignorantly like a shroud.

Jake is not surprised to find the address J-P gave him to be among the more decrepit houses on the street. Built, no doubt, by one of the faceless developers of the late nineteenth century. A utilitarian row house attached to the sidewalk with no balcony or portico, only side-by-side doors in an anonymous brick façade. Tall and thin. Falling face-first into the street. Even its windows look out onto the avenue with apathy.

It is early, he knows, but the echo of his rapping has barely died away before a face like a pale moon appears behind the shade., followed by the sound of locks snapping loose. Jake identifies each one unconsciously by its signature pop and grind—Chubb, Yale, Diebolt. The familiar noise settles his nerves.

"*Oui?*" The voice comes to him desperate and weak. Thin as the clothes on the woman's back. "*Je peux vous aider?*"

"Yes," Jake begins. "It's your husband."

"*Mon époux?*"

"*Oui, madame. J'ai une nouvelle de lui.*"

The door is open only to the extent of its chain. The woman wears a shapeless dress. Olive green. And down the front, a folded apron. Her hair is a shade of brown. Auburn. Naturally thick, but so long and heavy it does nothing but hang like a dish towel down her back. She is very thin. Jake can see this much in spite of the dress. She looks like none of the women Jean-Pierre described to him.

"*Mais je n'ai pas d'époux, monsieur. Vous vous trompez d'adresse, je crois.*"

And for a moment, Jake feels relieved. It was a con, after all. Mme Jean-Pierre Laroque does not exist. No one spent the night in useless vigil. But he must know for sure, and so he tries again.

"*Je parle, madame, de Jean-Pierre.*"

The change in the woman's expression is barely discernable. A ripple in the pond of her face. But it is there.

"*Entrez, s'il vous plait.*"

The young woman unfastens the last clasp dividing them and steps away from the door. A baby sits on her right hip, quietly watching. Its pale blue eyes are lined in red.

"Please. *Mon nom est Adèle,*" she says and turns to climb the steep inner staircase toward the second floor. She is barefoot, and Jake watches the red, calloused flesh of her heels as he follows.

A small living room lies to the right at the top of the stairs, adjoined to a windowless dining area. On the other side of the hallway is a bedroom. Jake is led past all this to the kitchen at the rear of the house, narrow as a railcar. A small window overlooks the shared yard. The outhouse. The laundry and the well. The woman lights the stove beneath a cold pot of coffee.

"Sit. Please," she says. And Jake takes up one of two straight-backed chairs around an ordinary gateleg table with both wings collapsed. The woman takes the other, switching the child to her lap.

"It was an accident?" Her voice does not betray emotion, but Jake can tell by her posture, erect and stiff, that she is steeling herself for the worst.

"Yes."

"At the factory?"

Jake is not trying to delay the news. He wants only to know what she knows, and the last question confirms that Jean-Pierre was keeping her in the dark.

"*Oui. À l'usine,*" he lies.

"*Et il est mort, mon frère?*"

The woman is unconsciously petting the head of the child in her lap. Smoothing the boy's burgeoning locks in a compulsive manner, rocking slightly with the motions of her hand.

"Oui." So it was a partial con. No wife. But a sister instead. Jake's voice is barely a whisper.

The woman looks to the floor. Her neck is flushed. No husband. No father. And now the brother is gone. The child's nose is running. Jean-Pierre was a stand-up guy in his own way. Just a loser looking out for his sister. The woman is crying inaudibly now.

"You . . . you worked with him?" She uses the end of her apron to wipe the child's nose. He fusses and also begins to cry half-heartedly. "Is . . . is there any money?" she continues. "*De la compagnie?*"

Jake does not hesitate. "Yes," he says. "Tomorrow, with the

regular pay." He glances around the shabby room, close as a closet. And dark, even at the break of day. When he stands, she does not look up. From the door he says, "*Désolé.*"

But she is staring out the window at the yard.

Jake leans against the traffic standard on the corner a block down from his apartment building. He is smoking a cigarette. The black sting of it in his chest. It is the only fag missing from the pack in his breast pocket. He thinks at that moment about the derailment of his life in the past few weeks. Not since the death of his wasted father has he been so sloppy and direction-less. He considers tossing the cigarette into the street and turn-ing away. The sister is none of his business. J-P made his own bed and almost sold Jake's out from under him. Even standing here is an unnecessary risk. He takes another drag from the foul-tasting butt and promptly exhales over his clothing.

Down the road, half-concealed in a portico, a man feigns interest in *The Gazette.* Jake has been watching him for a quar-ter of an hour. The man hasn't turned a single page. However, he does glance up and down the street regularly. It is almost noon. Several times, he has checked his watch. A police officer expecting relief. Ten minutes, he thinks.

Jake tosses the finished smoke down a sewer grill and reaches for the pack. With a fresh one between the tips of his fingers, he steps into the street, headed toward the cop. His heart beats like a pair of wings. The arteries beneath his ear course with adrenaline. The street is empty.

"*Pardon?*" he asks, brandishing the unlit cigarette and step-ping in close when he draws alongside the man with the newspaper. "*Avez-vous du feu?*"

The officer glances once in either direction and then folds
the paper under his arm. He is a rather big man with a pointy
face and loose skin beneath his chin. He is clean-shaven but
for a dark moustache. The tan fedora pulled low over his brow
makes him look more like a gangster than a cop. When he
reaches into his vest for the requested match, Jake catches a
glimpse of the shoulder strap. This is his man.

Jake delivers a quick jab with his splayed right hand. The
recess between his thumb and forefinger catch the man about
the throat. A cough escapes his parted lips before he crumples
to his knees, both hands reaching for his throat in reflex. Eyes
as round as pie plates. The newspaper and the box of matches
hit the ground on either side of him.

Jake kicks open the front entrance to the apartment block
immediately behind the cop and then pulls the wounded man
y the collar through to the foyer. The cop is still gasping for
air when Jake snatches the revolver from beneath his arm. He
tosses the firearm like a juggler and catches it by the barrel. In
the same motion he brings it down on the back of the man's
skull. The cop's arms fall away from his throat, and immediately his body becomes dead weight.

Jake slips the pistol down the front of his trousers and looks
up the stairwell to ensure no one is watching. Satisfied, he slides
an arm under each of the man's shoulders and drags him down a
flight of stairs to the basement, stowing him beneath the steps.

Outside, a vagrant searches through a trash can across the
street. Several other men have rounded the corner two blocks
down. Labourers from the Canadian Car and Foundry, Jake
guesses, on their way home for lunch. He is breathing heavily
and the blood in his ears drowns out all sense of sound. His
legs drag behind him like lead as he jogs across the street

toward his building. The bruised ribs will not allow him enough air. All the way across, Jake expects to hear the report of a pistol. Feel the blunt wreck of shell burrowing into the back of his head. The haunting peal of J-P's bullet plays over and over. But he makes the front entrance without incident.

He pauses inside the door, hands on his knees, heaving. Begging for air. Behind his eyes, last night's flight plays like a motion picture. Branches and roots reach for him. The desert of night extends outward from him like a shadow he can't shake.

He takes the first landing two steps at once, but by the time he reaches the top of the third flight, he is using the wall for support. The door to his apartment is slightly ajar, but no sound escapes. Jake draws the revolver as a precaution and proceeds slowly, creeping along the wall. Someone opens a door on the floor below. Jake waits until he hears the footfalls retreating down and away. He rounds the corner into his room just as his breath is finally returning.

The mattress has been tossed and slashed. His books are everywhere. The covers removed, pages torn. The magazines are the same. Houdini still looks down from above, only now, half his face is missing. Torn away and lying upside-down on the floor. His straitjacket is missing entirely. Quickly, Jake crosses the room and peers carefully through the window. No sign of anyone at the door across the way. Just the box of matches and the littered newspaper, blown open now, escaping down the street.

When Jake returns his gaze to the room, his throat tightens and he has to fight the urge to cry. Years of work and preparations toward a career as an escape artist have been violated. And he thinks fleetingly of his father then. In the years prior to the Jeffries fight. Bent over his own stone and pushing uphill.

The cache looks untouched, at least, although he barely wants to hope. On hands and knees, he draws back the board, and is relieved. Stuffing his pockets with renewed energy. As he does so, the noon whistle from the Canadian Car and Foundry blows clear up the stairwell into his room.

Over at the window again, he sees another suit stooped over the box of matches. He'll have to use the fire escape, he thinks.

Despite its attempt to appear otherwise, the St. Tropez borders on the seedy. A desirable quality in a nightclub. It gives the rich and not-so-famous a sense that they are slumming it with the Bohemians. Swilling bathtub gin in a New York speakeasy. Israel does his best to foster this illusion of decadence. All cocktails are served in teacups, and he himself carries a hollowed-out cane. In the few years since their installation, the zinc-plated bar fixtures have been battered and neglected. The low ceiling has developed mould and the already dark walls have attracted cigarette smoke like a shawl. The bathrooms are unmentionable.

When Jake enters, this time through the front door, the house band is playing "Black Bottom." Partygoers flood the dance floor. One woman lurches alone with her stockings turned down, powdered knees and bare arms flying. Her mouth is a bright red smear.

Jake feels like he has awakened from a long and dreamless sleep. The world is all angles and noise. Just above the dancers at the far end of the narrow room, he can read "Salle de

Billiards." Beyond, he can almost picture Israel's table with its chequered cloth over an inverted wine barrel. And Benji, close as a lapdog, only twice as ugly. But mostly Jake is thinking about women. Adèle in her threadbare tent and skinny arms. The chapped lips parting in a sigh as he hands her the mess of bills, repackaged in an envelope. And then there's Lulu, floating beyond the dancers like a freshly laundered sheet, trailing perfumed wind. Her blue eyes sharp as tacks. The languid body of a pregnant cat draped over Israel's shoulders. The loose breasts of a Botticelli, and dangerous legs like folded scissors.

He should be considering Israel's reaction, he knows, but he is lost in this paradox of women and wondering what it means to him, or why he cares at all. Israel will be an innundation when they meet. Plenty of time for that later. Jake turns to the small, covered bar and requests a drink.

"This one's on Israel," he says over the din, but he is not sure the bartender even cares. Israel got it all right with the St. Tropez. Down to the rude, moustachioed serving staff.

He leans back on the countertop, propped up on his elbows, and breathes in the room. A trio of men drinks outside Israel's door. Shaggy men with cigarettes and the potential of violence. Benji's army of replacements, biding time, he thinks. Israel's insurance policy.

Is this what awaits him? thinks Jake. Life as a glorified footman? He's broke now. Gave everything to Adèle. Not out of altruism. He's sure of that much. Perhaps it was shame, or simply a temporary loss of direction. Jake swallows the Scotch in a single go—a taste he acquired during his days as a burglar of fine things—and then slowly crosses the room.

The three toughs look up from their cigarettes, but only

half-heartedly. Sniffing. No bark. Jake has barely crested the threshold of the billiards room when Israel calls to him.

"Jacob. Come, come." To Jake's surprise, the man is standing, causing all sorts of commotion for those surrounding him in the booth. People file out and stand, including Benji, unsure whether they should take their seats again. Gawking like witnesses to an accident. Lulu is a cool drink in baby blue and diamonds. Israel breaks free of them, frustrated with his own lack of grace, and scowling.

He is wearing the signature white suit and matching patent leather shoes. A ring on every finger. His head arrives at Jake's chin.

"Louisa has told me everything. Everything." Israel waves his hands at the room, shakes his head. "The Frenchie. He is dead, yes?"

Jake nods, looking past his boss to the small, blinking crowd.

Israel turns to face the room. "This is a play for you? We are entertainment? Sit. Drink." He lays a hand on Jake's shoulder and directs him towards the rear of the club. Where the real money is made. Benji follows, but Israel calls him off.

"Louisa. Please."

Jake realizes that this is the first time he will enter a room with Israel alone, and even Benji seems confused. Eyes pinched in the folds of grey skin. But Lulu flows around the old toad like water moving downstream.

At the billiards table, on their way to the office, Jake sees Bobby leaning on a pool cue with his shirtsleeves rolled up. He watches the three pass with disturbing silence. A hooker leans in to kiss him just as Jake disappears through the metal door. Lulu is staring back.

Unlike the nightclub, Israel's office is Spartan. A replica of its warehouse cousin. A naked bulb burns above a bureau. Filing cabinets crammed in along one wall. A safe behind the desk. Israel leans over the expanse of wood toward Jake, his head like a chicken.

"They were real police officers?" he asks.

Jake can sense Lulu off in the shadows to his right. "State troopers, I think. Customs, maybe. Jean-Pierre tipped them off."

"Death becomes him, then." Israel retreats into his chair, each of his hands fingering the desktop. Eyes searching.

"You know, Jacob, this is bad news. The money alone . . . you couldn't even guess. But the customers, Jacob. That's the real problem. To whom do I sell now? We're not talking about a bathroom still. I make Seagrams blush." Israel raises his head. "What am I saying? Jacob, I'm happy to see you well. Not just for your dear, departed father, either. You're like a son to me. And Louisa, she would be devastated."

Jake's heart skips a beat. His throat constricts. How does he know?

"She's been bending my ear, *boyo*." Israel extends his manicured hand in Lulu's direction. She moves to it like a puppet. "She was quite an act, you know. The perfect assistant for a magic show, yes?" The man's sharp eyes look out from shadowed lids. Under the bulb, his face looks like a carnival poster for the haunted house.

"Mr. Karpowicz?"

"It's what you wanted. Am I right? The Amazing Jacobi." Israel sketches the headline in the air above them. "After all. You're a wanted man. What better cover than a public life?"

Jake allows himself to breathe.

Jake stares over Lulu's raised hip in the direction of the window. It is not yet dawn. The dimpled flesh is diffused by pale grey light. His head rests on the palm of his left hand. With the right, he reaches for the slope of her thigh, and she rolls toward him, startled by the touch. Her dark face smiling.

"I didn't know you were awake," she says.

Without answering, he tips her backward into the pillows. Crawling over her, Jake parts her long legs and settles himself between them. Hard but in no hurry.

"How did you do it?" he asks her. The question he's been wondering all night. Perhaps it is even part of the reason underlying his ardour.

Israel left the nightclub with Benji and all three toughs not long after he offered Jake the loan. Even now it seems unreal, except for the woman beneath him.

Everything had seemed to slip away from him over the last few weeks, as though his body had lost all gravitational force, sending his dreams careening outward into space. And then suddenly this.

Lulu arches her back beneath him, stretching like an exotic pet. The room around them is a Bedouin tent, draped in fine fabrics—her dress on the chair, the Persian carpet, and the Oriental drapes. Even the silk sheets beneath them. She renders the common glamorous, he thinks, as the fan pushes a wave of hot air over his back.

She need not answer the question, because Jake knows that he too would do anything she asked.

The Amazing Jacobi, 1930

Lulu is placed upon the board and fastened with leather restraints. Against Jake's wishes, she is scantily dressed in pink iridescent sequins and plumes. He makes a show of pulling the belts tight and invites a young man from the audience to test his work. The boy ascends to the stage amidst whistles and jeers. A man at the back yells lewd remarks concerning Lulu. The Central Canadian Exhibition is meant to be the highlight of their season. A season that began last winter with Jake's purchasing supplies with Israel's money and constructing many of the stage devices himself. They have now been touring for six months without a break, and they are haemorrhaging money.

It is the first time either of them has been in Toronto, and Jake has been awed by the crowds drawn to the fair. Only, he has been equally discouraged by attendance at their shows. Tomorrow night's performance will be their last, and they will be lucky to break even with the transportation costs and their room at the Royal York. Another of Lulu's indulgences. He has let go almost all his stagehands, hiring itinerant workers instead. A steadily growing social class, as it turns out.

Increasingly, Jake begins the show with Lulu in a quick series of illusions. Tired tricks. But the predominantly male audience appreciates them nonetheless. Tonight, they are performing early in an attempt to catch the after-dinner crowd, but there are many who have come straight from the beer halls instead.

When the boy is finished, he returns to the audience and Jake proceeds. Two of his hired hands carry Lulu toward the rear of the stage like stretcher bearers and place the board upon a specially crafted metal trestle. The entire set-up is encased in a cabinet of black cloth, the front of which is open. Lulu is then tipped forward at an angle so that the audience can see her. Whistles again. The man at the back bays like a dog in heat. Jake reaches into his breast pocket and withdraws a pistol. Lulu has no time to escape before he unceremoniously fires the gun into the cabinet.

In the great puff of smoke that ensues, the board comes crashing down upon the floor. Lulu has vanished.

In reality, the board is actually two boards. The one to which Lulu is attached has a mirror on the flip side. The other is a replica of the first, without the mirror. When Jake fires the gun, a stagehand sets in motion a complicated system of pulleys that swing Lulu around, one quarter revolution. At the same time, the replica drops. A combination of smoke and movement from the falling board confuse the audience sufficiently so that they do not notice Lulu turning away from them.

The two stagehands return quickly, gathering the board for the sake of the audience. It is indeed empty. The restraints dangle like atrophic limbs. But instead of applause, someone in the crowd yells, "Bring 'er back." And the others laugh.

Jake extends his hand toward the wing, and Lulu rejoins him at a quick step. The men erupt.

The show drags on interminably for Jake. Some of the legitimate patrons are forced to leave partway through, no longer able to put up with the rowdy house. And yet he continues putting Lulu to advantage with such illusions as the Floating Venus and Vanishing from the Ladder. Periodically, Jake will slip a cuff or perform rope tricks while the next illusion is set, but he ends each program with a different escape as the grand finale.

Tonight, he has opted for the Chinese Water Torture Cell.

The effects of the alcohol on the crowd are waning and the room is more subdued when the contraption is wheeled on stage. Jake built it himself. Even fashioned the metal pins that hold the glass cabinet together. It weighs half a ton with the water and takes every available stagehand to push it forward. Its low, grumbling approach stops even the most diehard heckler.

The cabinet resembles a phone booth or an upright sarcophagus, and its conglomeration of glass and burnished steel conjures images of mad Dr. Frankenstein's laboratory. As an added bit of showmanship, Jake undresses on the stage—down to his briefs, his lean frame gleaming under old-fashioned gaslights. Unlike the cuff and rope tricks, this escape will take place out of the audience's sight. Once he is inside, Lulu will draw back a curtain and pace the stage with a pocket watch, calling out each half-minute Jake remains submerged.

The greatest challenge facing Jake in this stunt is remaining inverted underwater while a set of ankle restraints is bolted into place. Lulu accomplishes this with surprising speed. It's something they practise repeatedly. The sight of Jake squirming like a pickled lab rat mesmerizes the members of the audience. And for the sixty seconds it takes Lulu to bolt and secure the remaining locks on the outside of the tank, their eyes remain glued to the merman wafting weightless as a helium balloon.

Sixty peaceful seconds when Jake has nothing to do but wait and think. About the failure of his first season. Lulu's cold rebuff each night after the show. Her periodic disappearances, sometimes for days. Sixty seconds before the curtain is drawn to separate him from the audience. Sixty seconds before he can begin the process of escape.

For all its wondrous mechanics, the torture chamber is a relatively simple illusion. The trick is in the lungs. Outlasting the process of confinement while the crowd is privy to his drowning. Once they can no longer see him, Jake has only to bend at the waist and unfasten the bolts at his ankles. And after his head discovers its original equilibrium, he has only to repeat the process with the tank's rigged lid.

Music plays throughout the attempt, and, to heighten the illusion's effect, Jake stands dripping by the chamber's grotesque statuary for an additional minute before the curtain is removed. The man's showmanship comes into play then. Chest heaving, shoulders slumped. Arms like dead fish at his sides.

Jake listens to the music coming distorted through the water. Remains suspended for moments after the curtain is drawn, concentrating on the dull ache in his chest. Already the escape is old. Not at all as he had anticipated. Lulu will be posing beyond the cloth wall, calling time at regular intervals according to a pocket watch. The crowd talking indiscriminately, almost oblivious. And if he were to fail, he thinks. Hold out to the last second and then die in the attempt? Would they understand then?

Jake reaches up to unthread the first bolts at his feet. The left foot swings free in seconds. But the next bolt is jammed. Threaded improperly, carelessly by Lulu. Jake employs both hands to the task, but the screw will only move a half turn more before sticking hopelessly in the unoiled socket. The loss of his permanent stage crew is beginning to manifest itself in the act. Last week a jammed pulley during a dry run of The Transformation Cabinet. And now this. His earlier hesitation has come back to haunt him, as well. The burn in his lungs is much greater now.

The hired hands are pooled backstage, listening to a story, their backs to Jake. The show is drawing to a close and already their minds are elsewhere. A wall lies between him and Lulu. Jake abandons the screw and reaches out for the bolts on the tank lid. He presses his one free leg against the glass for leverage, relieving the strain on his abdomen. Surely, he thinks, Lulu will wonder at the extra time.

The six bolts pop free with relative ease, but Jake's right foot is still attached, the lid shut. He forces the metal stopper to the edge of the tank so that a third of it hangs over the side. Jake can see a crack of light now, almost ten inches wide. His head swimming, eyes losing focus with the lack of oxygen. With his free left foot, Jake kicks the lid upward, but not forcefully enough. It comes crashing back against the tank. The stagehands look over their shoulders, realization blooming slowly. Jake kicks, flails at the lid again. Just enough to spill it over the side this time. Pain shoots through his right ankle as it slides, yanking him out of the water with its weight, twisting his leg. Both hands can reach the top of the tank now and he pulls himself to the surface. A ladder rattles against the glass then. A man scampers up the side. Jake can feel the urgent grasp of fingers on his arm. The two others cradle the lid, easing the pain in his leg. Air bursts through his teeth like a cannon. The music sharpens into tight lines as he surfaces, throwing water over the stage.

A moment later he is on the floor. Water cascading. The lid like a ball and chain. Jake waves off the stagehands and orders the curtain open. The audience is revealed to him in a rush. Lulu in pink feathers, smiling. There is applause, but it is not thunderous. Not nearly enough. Jake lowers one knee to the stage. A moment later his head bows, and the crowd files out into the warm night air. Seeking the midway.

Jake sits backstage with his leg up. A bag of ice on his ankle. The hired help has been paid and they are already populating the drinking holes.

"I don't see why you are angry with me," says Lulu, producing a cigarette now that they are alone. "How this is my fault?" In the bad lighting she looks like a poorly plucked chicken with good legs. Lulu lights the cigarette and blows smoke into the air above them.

"I'm not pointing fingers," says Jake, feeling suddenly very tired.

"You don't need to. I know that look."

This is becoming all too common, he thinks. He has lived alone for so long that he has grown to appreciate silence, and this constant rehashing of events and emotions is draining for him. And each time he tries to reach out, to find the right words, things only get worse.

"It's just . . ."

"What? It's just what?"

"This." Jake extends his arms, indicating the world around them. "It isn't working. It's not how I imagined it."

Lulu looks away. "You're not Houdini," she says.

"What?" Jake can hear a buzzing in the back of his head. His cheeks are hot.

"You're not," she repeats. "And this isn't 1907. Today a woman flew a biplane over the fairgrounds, turning rolls as she passed. She was so close to the crowd you could see her smile."

"What are you saying? That I should take up flying?"

Lulu shakes her head. Blows smoke though pursed lips. "I'm saying this isn't enough. Not any more."

Jake thinks back to the last escape. What else can he do?

Jake spies him amongst the flood of people at the midway. It isn't the first time. Twice before, he was sure it was him, but each time, he slipped away. And Lulu only raged when he'd confronted her. But this time, there is no mistaking him. The slight body and affected dress of a dandy. He's wielding a pellet gun at the shooting gallery and doing quite well, Jake realizes. But he is too infuriated to be impressed. He sets his teeth and acts without thinking. The pain in his ankle fires like a piston, but he ignores it, bumping and pushing his way through the sea of bodies between himself and his quarry. Unwilling to lose him this time.

"Bobby," he says with no particular malice, and the boy swings in his direction.

Jake lands a quick punch, pulling it only slightly, square in the kid's diaphragm. And with his right hand, disarms him, dropping the gun on the counter.

"Hey," says the carnie, as Jake leads Bobby away by the ear. "You gonna pay for him?"

But Jake is out of earshot almost immediately, shoving the boy in amongst the trailers. When he is released, Bobby falls to all fours, gasping.

"What are you doing here?" Jake spits, looming above his heaving form, tattooed with bands of light from the Ferris wheel overhead.

He wants to press him further, to pummel him, actually. As a scapegoat, if nothing else. For his own failure as a performer. For Lulu. But before he can do anything, the boy moves. If he had attempted something more furtive, he might even have succeeded. Only, Jake catches the rapid movement of the boy's hand, the appearance of bright steel, just in time to feint away. The pain erupts in his ankle in response to the awkward reaction. Lights pop behind his eyes and he collapses.

Somewhere above him, Jake hears a knife sink into wood. There is no point in standing. He knows the boy is gone.

Six miles in 7 minutes, 37 seconds.

Houdini was born to fly. To break the laws of gravity and escape the earth. He was the first successful aviator on the Australian continent. Lost to the crowd at Digger's Rest for more than seven minutes. Battling a cross-current of violent air in his Voisin biplane. The object of adoration for more than thirty onlookers, including the Consul for the Italian Touring Club.

More than one hundred feet above the broiled plain, he kept his goggled eyes upon the ever far horizon, thinking even then of Tennyson's "Ulysses." If he could do this upon a skeleton of matchstick wings and paper, what next?

> *Come, my friends.*
> *'Tis not too late to seek a newer world.*
> *Push off, and sitting well in order smite*

The sounding furrows; for my purpose holds
To sail beyond the sunset, and the baths
Of all the western stars, until I die.

Dreams of the Hippodrome, the Olympic Music Hall, and
the Orpheum in New Orleans seem naïve in the face of
Jake's current reality. A rundown hotel room in Niagara
Falls, Ontario. Walls so thin they're practically translucent
and full of the sounds of newlyweds fucking. Lulu has abandoned him yet again, choosing instead a single at the
Regency that they cannot afford. The fragile threads of
their relationship have been unravelling rapidly since
Toronto. He has told her nothing about Bobby and is
almost ashamed of himself. His world is a carousel flinging
horses into space, or a spinning top on the verge of wobble.
Beyond his window, gaslights illuminate the falls, and its
great, roaring rush is a backdrop to the human grunt and
groan of the walls around him.

The crowds here are equally sparse and only slightly more
receptive. But it is a city bored with daring and acts of singular
bravado. A city rich in inadvertent suicides. Rusted barrel
rings silt the bottom of the whirlpool like tiny mouths frozen
in the round expression of surprise. And it was in Niagara
Falls that the Great Farini made his name astride a tightrope.
A mad and drunken march over the void with only the body's
penchant for balance to protect him.

These are the men Jake understands. The last of the living
in a world leaning toward parlours and teacups. He never saw
Farini's act, but the man's legend is enough for Jake. To know
that he is not alone. There were others before him who

understood the spiritual nature of risk, the adrenaline temptation and the holy communion of the spectacle.

Jake remembers the last time he saw Houdini's act in Montreal. The Princess Theatre, 1926. Only days before the man's innocuous death. He had become a name by then. An entry in every English dictionary. Crowds of thousands flocked to see him perform on Broadway, a show that ran two weeks. No longer a man tricking congregations outside dime store museums, Houdini had become a magician and the centre of a one-man travelling storm. Two hours he mesmerized the packed house of the Princess.

Amusing them at first with card tricks, sleight of hand. Moving next to Spiritualists, exposing their methods in elaborate schemes. But eventually he came around to his hallmark displays of escape. Handcuffs and ropes. And, to Jake's delight, a recreation of the East River Escape. A life come full circle for a twelve-year-old boy perched upon his father's shoulders.

And yet, even then, Jake could see the man was hurting. A workhorse straining against the failure of his lungs and the atrophy and aging muscles. It was beautiful. The dying light of a crimson sunset.

The mythology around those last few days was quick to form after the man's collapse in Detroit. The world wanted more than appendicitis. It wanted a fifteen-round technical knockout. Axes cleaving into the last milk can. Bronze coffins inches too deep in the earth. A final hopeless kick at the dark.

Jake lies on his back and considers the ceiling. Thinks of the way the world unconsciously understood the artist's quest. And he tries to comprehend why it cannot recognize his own as one and the same. Perhaps Lulu is right. The world does not want another Houdini. The ante is up. The stakes have been raised. Houdini was a man of his times, but the times have changed.

Men are fighting their own battles. The demons of unemployment and incomprehensible economics. What is the place of a man in all this? What is the battlefront? The enemy is indistinguishable, a concept without a shape. When law and order civilized America, Houdini slipped their cuffs and escaped from their jails. When vulgar death swept through Europe in the guise of war, Houdini tempted it. And when soaring concrete towers clouded the skylines of New York and Chicago, blocking out the sun, Houdini hung from them like a bat.

What would he have done in the face of unemployment lines and empty factories? Jake wonders. Crashing markets and the heartless hunger of foreclosing banks?

Jake sits up in his bed. His mind reels with the thought. Suddenly, it's there before him. His next escape.

Jake whispers his idea into Lulu's ear and a week later they are back in Montreal. The St. Tropez is oddly calm and the backroom is a morgue, but inside Israel's office, Lulu is ebullient. She lays herself across the mobster's knee like a child with her Christmas wish list. Benji looks as interested as a corpse, but Israel is responsive. Definitely engaged.

"So let me get this straight. You want to rob a bank." Israel is addressing Jake, but his eyes are all over Lulu. One hand cupping her chin.

"Well, yes. And no," answers Jake. "It's a stunt. Like Houdini's jailbreak ..."

"Yes, yes. Forget about Houdini."

"The city, the whole country's angry. They're losing their

jobs. The bank is calling in loans. Foreclosing on homes and farms."

"So?"

Lulu is feeding the man peanuts. His interjections come monosyllabic through mouthfuls.

"So we harness that anger. We convince a bank to lock me in its vault. Invite the press. Advertise in the papers. 'One Thousand Dollars for the Crowd.' When I escape with the money, I'll scatter it among the audience. You can't buy better publicity."

"One thousand dollars?" Israel repeats. "You are buying publicity. Am I right?"

"Sponsors," Jake adds. "You canvass area businesses for the cash. It's advertising for them too. They're hurting. Nothing's moving and no one is buying. It'll be a carnival. We could issue an open challenge."

"And me? You need something from me?" Israel looks at Jake for the first time and then back to Lulu.

"You're the money, honey." Lulu takes his face in her hands and kisses Israel on the mouth.

Jake shifts in his chair. "Well, the means to the money, anyway. You've got ..."

"Connections," says Lulu.

She has him, Jake thinks. The man can't say no to her.

"You can do this, Jacob? Escape from a bank vault?"

Last week on the road, he and Lulu talked of nothing but the Bank Vault Escape. However, their conversation skirted the details of its presentation to Israel. Not once has Jake considered the technical obstacles. So he lies.

"Yes. I can."

"Then why stop at one thousand dollars?"

The question catches Jake completely by surprise. He can

feel the eyes of Benji and Lulu just as intent as the mobster's before him.

"Excuse me?"

"There's a lot of money in a bank vault. Cash. Jewellery. Bearer's Bonds. A quarter of a million at least," Israel says. "Wouldn't you agree, Benji?" Israel looks over his shoulder at the mummified gangster against the back wall.

"Maybe more." His voice is a dull cough, like dust blown off a seldom-used instrument.

"Maybe more," Israel repeats. "The thing is, Jacob, it's a tough time for everyone. Capone says he don't know what street Canada is on. A funny one, that. But my operation is a shambles since that little Frenchman screwed things up last fall. And this business with the market. Jacob, I have creditors. And I have debtors." His gaze takes on a more sinister appearance. Weight. "A quarter of a million dollars goes a long way, Jacob. And your share, well, that would wipe the slate clean between you and me. With more than a little left over."

"Think about it, Jake." Lulu's voice comes to him like a cold bucket of water. She doesn't appear surprised at all by Israel's suggestion. Sits like a queen in his lap. "That's a lot of money."

And then it hits him. Lulu is a dangerous woman. That's all part of the attraction.

It is already late when Jake leaves the St. Tropez alone. Ste. Catherine is almost deserted but for a few desperate men and women lurking in the darker doorways. Jake turns corner after corner, unconsciously seeking the mountain. His head is full of demons as he climbs the streets of Mt. Royal, through the university and up the darkened forest trails to the belvedere.

For the first time, he understands his father. The cage the man lived in. Hemmed in by poverty, illiteracy, and men like Israel Karpowicz. The puppeteers who pull the strings. As a child, Jake thought he had the world figured out, and he lived under that illusion until this evening. His father was an embarrassment next to Israel. Or so he thought. But he was a man who truly lived. By his wits and by his hands. While he had the use of them. Only, it's a difficult life once you find the extent of your cage in each direction, and then realize that the effort to escape takes more than you have in you. The worst part, Jake thinks, is that throwing in the towel only hastens the end. He saw this in his father. The man was never the same after the Jeffries fight.

Jake, too, lost direction then, ending up in a different sort of cage. Fortunately, he was young and escape was still an option. But then perhaps he has been too preoccupied with escape. Mistaken its challenge as the only possible life. Is J-P's sister not living? Facing the darkness of her cage with just as much bravado? Certainly more than Israel and Lulu. Than Benji. Maybe Houdini realized that as well. Perhaps that is the difference between the artist and himself. Houdini understood that in facing down the cold reality of your cage, in attempting an escape, you must also admit defeat. Outside every cage there is another waiting. And so you must agree to accept that and live anyway. Not in ignorance. But in conscious acquiescence.

Easier said than done, however. Israel is the keeper of his cage, and Lulu thinks she can cross effortlessly between captor and captive. Jake is certain he can escape from the bank vault.

But he is not convinced he can escape Israel, or that he wants to escape from Lulu at all.

Montreal lies beneath him like a carpet of light and dark. The orthogonal grid of gaslit streets, its delicate warp and weft. And the ocean-going vessels slipping quietly through the river, like the shuttle on a loom, introducing new threads.

It is almost dawn when he returns to her apartment and finds an empty bottle of champagne. Two glasses. He was right, then, not to return earlier. Though part of him hopes to find Israel even now. Curled into Lulu and dreaming. To force a confrontation he is otherwise unable to initiate. But he knows that she will be alone from habit.

Jake pulls up a wingbacked chair by the bed and watches Lulu turned into her sleep. Foetal hands on the pillow. Her breath only a whisper. But even like this she seems invulnerable. No trace of innocence in the lines of her face. Hers is the sound sleep of the strategos whose plans are fully realized. And yet Jake finds it impossible to be angry with her betrayal.

Long after the sun has risen and Jake has slipped into his own dreams, he is awakened by the sound of her voice pulling him toward consciousness.

"Jake," she says, hands extended from the folds of a silk robe, an oriental print of spare trees and elegant women. She holds a coffee cup out to him, the smell acrid and familiar. He takes it grudgingly and sits up stiff in the chair.

"Where did you go last night?" she asks. "I had champagne." Lulu sits on the edge of the unmade bed. Tips the hot liquid past her lips.

"And someone else to share it with." Jake tries to sound angry, but comes up short. Petulant at best.

Lulu only blinks in response.

"How could you do this to me?" he asks.

"Do?" There's something more than confusion in her gaze, but Jake presses on.

"You suggested the robbery to Israel."

"No," she answers with finality.

"But you supported the idea."

"I did nothing to discourage it. I thought you'd be happy."

"Happy?" Jake places the coffee cup on the night table and then stands.

"Yes. After this you can do whatever you want. Be your own boss. I thought that's what you were after." Lulu turns her head, following Jake as he paces around the bed.

"I'll be a criminal," he shouts at her from across the room, as though that explains everything.

"That's a stretch," she adds, withdrawing her gaze and following his lead. When she rounds the edge of the bed, her jaw is set. "You do nothing but complain for months about owing Israel, about Israel's interference. We'll be free, Jake. We can go anywhere."

"In hiding," he volleys. His dreams slip away from him like moons losing their orbit.

"Don't be ridiculous. We can start again, if that's what you want. A different name. A different place." She moves closer and lays her hands on his sleeve. Turns up his hand into hers. The soft insistence of it.

"Forget about Israel, Jake. We can keep it for ourselves. Go to Mexico, Jake. Cuba." And the word drops like an apple from a tree, brilliant and tempting.

"You've already made plans," he says. But the edge is gone from his voice. He sounds only tired now. "I don't need this money, Lulu. I can do this on my own."

"Your own," she says quietly. "What about me?" Lulu shakes herself free of him.

And for the first time he sees her in a new light. Failed actress. Kept woman. The lady in waiting. And he has nothing left to say.

It is only a matter of days before Israel finds an interested bank. A fledgling branch of the Caisse Desjardins in Laval. It happens so quickly that Jake does not have the time to back out. Like a train gathering steam, he is carried along by the plan's inertia. Lulu has returned to him as she was before. His nights are once again filled with the scent of her. And now that his mind is bent to the task, apprehension fades into the background. The details of the bank job draw his attention like a lodestone.

His talk before Israel had been full of confidence and bravado, but the reality of vault escape is anything but simple. Not even Houdini had ever successfully beat the bank. His only attempt had risen in the form of a similar challenge. An institution in London, England, responded to the man's invitation. Dared him to try his hand at their vault. And, of course, he had accepted. The date was set, and the band played a waltz while Houdini fretted from inside. In the past, using magnets, Houdini had been able to escape from even the toughest safe. But the vault proved itself beyond the master. For almost an hour the magician pitted himself against the door's mechanism. The task exhausted him. Down to his shirtsleeves and suspenders, he slumped against the unforgiving mass, considering the imminent possibility of failure. But chance loves the under-dog. The weight of his defeated frame pushed the door open on its balanced hinges. Feckless, it swung into the lobby of the tuxedo-clad waltzers. Each of their faces like the birth of a dream.

In all the confusion of the surrounding fanfare, no one had remembered to bolt the door into place. It was a secret Houdini carried with him for years.

Jake, however, can not base his success on the possibility of incompetence, so he decides to open a joint account at Des-jardins Laval the very next week.

Lulu jumps at the opportunity to take part in the ruse, to act the part of society matron. She even elects to go shopping for the occasion. Trades in her gowns for sensible skirts and shoes. White gloves and a wide-brimmed hat. The transfor-mation is startling for Jake and he, too, is fitted for a suit. In the full-length mirror in her room, they are the very picture of respectability. The banker doesn't stand a chance against Mr. and Mrs. Arnold Rump.

Arm in arm, the couple enters the Caisse at precisely ten o'clock on a Thursday morning. The bank occupies the ground floor of a three-storey building facing the street. From outside, it is anonymous grey brick. Inside, the lobby is equally unassuming. Open concept interrupted by wood-panelled support columns and waist-high oak cubicles. A row of cashiers are lined up across the wall.

The man who greets them is small and quick. The thick lenses of his wire-rimmed spectacles cause his eyes to widen like balloons from certain angles. He is the manager and will be han-dling their induction personally. Over the phone, Lulu intimated a certain wealth and the manager responds as they expected.

"Perhaps a tour," he suggests, and Lulu takes up his hand like an offering. She coos over the decor appropriately, throwing Jake an occasional comment that becomes a question with the casual addition of *isn't that right, darling?* or, *wouldn't you agree, dear?*

"He's the strong, silent type," she tells the manager at one point, and, after Jake requests to see the vault, she adds, "so practical."

Jake is amazed with her performance. Stunned into silence, not by nerves, but by the sheer wonder at her ability to shed skin and step into another like an old coat.

"All our deposit boxes are in here," the manager says as he pulls back the steel door. A Diebold, Jake registers. And inside, one entire wall is fitted with key-operated deposit boxes.

"Is this where my money will be kept?" Lulu asks, indicating a dull grey Herring-Hall and Marvin at the rear of the vault.

"A safe within a safe," says the man, smiling. "And any valuables over here."

Jake absorbs the room. Eight by twelve feet with ten-foot ceilings. The door is at least thirty-eight inches across, eighty-two tall with massive tube hinges. The whole mechanism is operated by a six-spoked captain's wheel on the outside, driving six individual metal bolts three inches in diameter. Two into either side of the door. One up. One down. A formidable piece, perhaps a ton all told. Locked with a forbidding combination release.

"Very impressive," he tells the manager.

Lulu smiles. "You have some paperwork for us to sign, no doubt."

Israel handles the stunt like a prizefight. The whole block is to be sealed off from traffic. A bandstand will be towed in on the back of a truck. It is to be a happening. A spectacle. He even has tickets printed and sold for a cocktail party in the bank's lobby while Jake attempts the escape. The haberdashery across the street plans an end-of-season sale to coincide with the event. But all this is arranged from a distance. Through channels and associates Jake cannot even begin to guess at. The trail back to Israel is covered in dust.

Everything is in place, but Jake. At his request, Israel orders in a replica of the vault door from the recently bankrupt Cleveland Trust Building and has it installed in his warehouse in the harbour. Jake spends a day just looking at it. Another just listening with his ear pressed up against the mechanics of it. Opening and closing. The safe deposit boxes and the Herring are nothing to him. But the vault is a dark cloud. The problem is its lack of features. All the hardware is fixed on the outside of the door. The inner panel is three inches of solid steel, blank as a cheque.

Around him, swallows dart in the rafters, their economic movements like caged chaos. He has not eaten in days. Lulu came around in the early going, but he only ignored her and, when that didn't work, he asked her to arrange for a getaway car. For once, Jake is happy at her extended absence.

Two days before the escape, the sky is cloud-covered, threatening rain. The old warehouse feels like an abandoned tomb, raided by oblivious generations of thieves. The only light bleeds in through holes in the tin roof where the swallows escape and return. Two days away and still no plan, he thinks. Jake can see the demons flitting in the gloom of the warehouse. Gathering outside the last vestiges of light. He has stared at the door for so long that the world has seemed to disappear, and now slowly it re-enters his conscious mind like water through a splintered dyke. Memories, too, bleed in on him in his exhaustion. His father dancing in the dark. Drifting, swinging at shadows. And he, alone and watching with heavy lids. Before the East River. Before Houdini. And before that last fight when everything changed.

Jake lies back on the cool cement of the warehouse floor and closes his eyes. He could leave, he thinks. Like his father did after the fight. He could walk out the gaping mouth of the warehouse and not look back. Or perhaps he could have done once, before Lulu. When he opens his eyes, the swallows are there, burning their white bellies in the black of the rafters— turning heroically at the last possible second and disappearing through the roof into a small island of sky.

And Jake cannot suppress his own smile in spite of everything. In spite of the darkness. His eyes locked on the brilliant flight of a swallow. The light at the end of his tunnel.

Mr. Arnold Rump pays a visit to his bank just a day before the escape. He wishes to leave a package in his safe deposit box. It is wrapped in brown paper and bound with a string. He smiles for the cashier, his false beard itching.

"Houdini Exposes the tricks used by the Boston Medium Margery."

Houdini was an illusionist, a man of tricks and sleight of hand. His performances were a matter of pride—the reason he published pamphlets and articles revealing the genius of his fictions from time to time. The tricks were not without danger, but he was sure to have the cards stacked in his favour. The mark of a good illusion was the audience's suspension of disbelief. But Houdini hated a chiseller, and the latter half of his career was spent exposing them. Spiritualists in particular.

Mina Crandon, known only as Margery, was his most infamous exposé. Channelling the dead went against everything he believed. It ridiculed his philosophy. His crusade eventually cost him many prominent friendships, including that of Sir Arthur Conan Doyle. But he was vindicated in the end by the publishers of the Scientific American. *The spiritualist methods became a part of his theatre thereafter, a reminder that there was only one way to linger after death, and that was to make your mark while alive. To burn out like a sun in sparks of hydrogen gas. To exit supernova.*

The crowd is already in the hundreds when Jake arrives by car. Camera flashes pop like champagne corks and blind him momentarily as he pushes through newsmen on his way to the bank. Their questions land like tossed coins at his feet.

"Is this some kind of political statement, Mr. Jacobi?"

"Has anything like this ever been successfully attempted?"

"Mr. Jacobi, do you consider yourself the next Houdini?"

"No." Jake answers to the last question but means it to answer all their queries.

The crowd, held back by ropes slung along a path to the main entrance, reaches out to him. They cheer and shout words of encouragement.

"Take it all," he hears distinctly from a man in the thick of them, just before he reaches the doors and disappears inside.

The little bank manager is a flurry of activity, clearing the way of well-dressed men and women. With a perturbed wave, he silences the band in the middle of "Bye, Bye, Blackbird."

"A photo," he says aloud to no one in particular, searching the flood of faces for a photographer and finding one, pulling him forward to where he and Jake stand as in a parted sea.

The little man seems not to recognize Mr. Rump at all. His identity is obscured by the smooth skin of a close shave and the curtain of circumstance. The mayor and several other local dignitaries vie for similar treatment and, for several minutes, Jake is occupied with posing and the shaking of hands.

The vault has been open all day for the viewing pleasure of the crowd. At fifteen cents a head, the bank has made a good profit. Eventually, Jake makes his way to the mouth of the vault and pauses for effect. He addresses the spectators who have filled in behind him like a wake.

"I will need an hour. No more. After such time, you may open the door yourselves and I will have failed. Be timely. I have not calculated the volume of oxygen in there and I shall be working strenuously."

At this last mention of oxygen, the audience is abuzz with talk. Jake turns from them and enters the vault. It closes behind him with a dull suck, followed by the fluid shush of multiple metal cylinders slipping into place. And so it begins.

Jake produces a lock pick from his pocket. As he suspected, the manager failed to consider this as a potential threat, the main door being impervious to such a device. From under his shirt and about his waist, he produces a canvas duffle bag. Quickly and efficiently, Jake empties each and every safe deposit box of its transferable valuables. Jewellery. Foreign currency. Coin collections and bonds. Items they can move readily in any city. Fifteen minutes later, the bag is filled close to capacity.

The band is only a dull hum from inside the vault, but Jake can pick out the bars of "Ain't We Got Fun" as he presses his ear to the door. The next step is the safe. Only a matter of practise, really. A thing he used to do when he was a burglar. Spilling the contents of wall-mounted strong boxes, ridiculously covered by art. Leaving enigmatic notes about the invented lovers of spouses. Careful listening. Trial and error. But time is pressing, and the greatest obstacle is nerve. Quietly Jake turns the dial clockwise. After a few minutes, he tries the release. But nothing happens. Jake takes a deep breath and leans into the mass of the safe. Closing his eyes, he begins again. Twenty-eight minutes in, the door swings out, revealing bundles of cash. Series of coin. He does not stop to count it out.

A moment later, the bag is full.

With just under thirty minutes left, Jake must turn his mind toward escape. There is only one safe deposit box remaining. For this one, he has the key. In it is the brown paper package he left only the day previous, winking suggestively at the cashier who blushed. Inside, he finds exactly what he needs. A hammer. A chisel. And a small handsaw.

Jake takes a step back from the tools and looks to the safe. Just the right height, he thinks. And then, Jake looks up at the ceiling. Considers the best place to begin.

A challenge.

Houdini had a running challenge. As early as 1900, he was bored with his own prowess and begging for the possibility of failure. He could escape from anything, he claimed. And inventors crawled from the woodwork to test him. In Blackburn, England, a fellow named Hodysen produced a set of irons that almost stumped the young magician. Two hours he laboured, but eventually prevailed, bloody and exhausted. His body prey to welts and purple bruises.

At the Hippodrome in London, he picked up another gauntlet. This time, The Mirror commissioned a blacksmith from Birmingham. The handcuffs he produced were designed with a series of Bramah locks—impossible to pick. But after weeks of hype and advanced publicity, Houdini shook them to the ground like a harmless second skin in less than an hour.

The closest he ever came to failure was in Milwaukee at the bottom of a sealed keg. What should have been a simple modified milk can escape almost saw him drowned. He had failed to calculate the chemical properties of the beer and ran too low on oxygen as a result. But in the end, no container could hold him. He was like water slipping into cracks and expanding like ice. He blew his prisons at the moon.

Jake is covered in plaster dust and flecks of lathe as he pulls himself up into the empty office above the vault. The duffle bag is slung about his shoulders. As he suspected, the band playing in the next room has masked the noise of his renovations. But there is precious little time remaining. A quick glance out the window of the office across the hall reveals the crowd restless with anticipation. They are pressed close to the ropes that keep them from the bank. Some stand on the tips of their toes, hoping for a better angle. Children are draped over their fathers' shoulders, shouting down details.

It is time, he thinks.

Jake passes noiselessly down the corridor toward the fire escape. At the bottom is the alley. And at the end of the alley is Lulu in a rented car. Waiting.

He can almost not believe his luck when he finds the alley empty but for trash and a stray cat mewling. His heart jumps, however, when at the far end where he is to exit, he spies a figure smoking. But when he realizes that the silhouette is Lulu, Jake smiles.

She turns, as if drawn by his sudden movement. Waves him on and drops the cigarette beneath the toe of her shoe.

"What are you doing out of the car?" Jake asks, breathless with his exertion and the adrenaline of his escape.

Lulu throws her arms around him in an embrace and then looks backward over her shoulder where an automobile sputters into being.

"Now, don't be cross with me, Jake."

He can barely trust his eyes as they come to rest on the chauffeur. Dark hair and swarthy good looks.

"We needed him, Jake. I can't drive."

Bobby pilots the car like an aeroplane through the streets. Banking the car around corners like it was floating.

"Slow down, for crissakes! Are you trying to get us stopped?" Jake yells into the front seat. The space between Lulu and the boy.

But Bobby only looks back with a sneer. "You wanna get out?

Just say so," he spits. The vulgar hatred burning in his small, fragile face.

Lulu reaches across and lays her hand on his forearm. The tense muscles relax and the car settles into a more acceptable speed.

After a moment of petulant silence, Jake says, "Why didn't you tell me that you couldn't drive? Didn't you think that was important?"

"Don't yell at her," Bobby says in a threatening monotone, staring up into the rearview mirror.

"Jesus," Jake breathes and sits back in the seat.

"How much do you suppose there is?" Lulu says and turns to lean into the back. Jake almost wants to smile at the way she is dressed. A flowered kerchief tied around her head and fastened at the neck. Dark glasses.

"Enough," he says instead.

Lulu beams and then crawls over the seat to join him. Bobby only scowls as Lulu's feet kick the air by his ear and then disappear as she tumbles into Jake's lap.

"I knew you could do it," she says after kissing him.

"Don't celebrate just yet," Jake cautions. But his body sends out a different message. He is practically vibrating with excitement. The money. The brilliant escape. The foiling of Israel's plan. Even Bobby's presence cannot ruin his high.

"The two of you can drive in shifts," Lulu adds, ignoring his outward pessimism. "We'll be in New Orleans by this time tomorrow."

"New Orleans? I thought we had decided on Cuba." Jake looks first at Bobby, who is staring furtively at him through the mirror. Then to Lulu.

"We are. We'll catch a ship over from there," she says.

"Yes. But why New Orleans? Why not Florida?"

"I've never been to New Orleans."

"Have you ever been to Florida?"

"Jake, honestly. We're rich and I want to spend my money in New Orleans." Lulu lays her head in Jake's lap. "The French Quarter. Royal Street."

Jake pulls his fingers through her hair. "Chicken Jambalaya," he adds.

"Now you're talking."

Jake returns to the river. Outside the automobile's dark rush, the world is black. His eyes close and he is twelve again. New York. The East River. Only, something is wrong this time. Houdini is lost to him. The crowd milling awkwardly. Three minutes elapse. Four. When the official timepiece reads five, people are talking. Worry sets in.

"Pull him up," says a woman.

At six minutes the protests increase. A man tries to muscle his way to the front, only to be stopped by cooler heads.

"For the love of God," shouts another. The organizers are huddled together by the banks. Jake strains to hear what they are saying, but the men speak in hushed tones.

His father stirs beneath him. "This don't look good."

Finally, the handlers come to life. Break off and begin the complicated process of raising the crate. In the haste, a line jams. Somebody swears.

"Faster," a man shouts. "He hasn't got any air." And even the obvious seems portentous.

When the box breaches the surface and pulls away, dripping, several bystanders reach out to aid the artist's assistants, trying desperately to bring the cargo to earth. No movement could be fast enough for them.

As the box touches down on the edge of the pier, the crowd presses in around the spectacle. Even Jake's father jockeys for position. Jake, himself, is torn between the urge to look away and the need to see. To know for sure. He recognizes the emotion as a battle between hope and fear. One of the organizers passes up a crowbar to the policeman hovering above the likely coffin. He prises nails and splits wood.

When the lid peels back, men rush in like water. For a moment, Jake loses sight of the crate beneath a sea of rescuers. But when they lay the body down, bloated and limp beside its ruined sarcophagus, he is shocked to see that it is his own.

Air crashing in through the driver's side window is just barely enough to keep Jake awake. His is the graveyard shift. They bought a map in Pennsylvania, but the car is a dark bubble hurtling through night. The map lies on the floor, partially folded and completely wrinkled. He travels by instinct, allowing the road to guide him. Lulu sleeps with her head against the passenger window. Bobby is stretched out in the back. Alone with his thoughts, Jake shifts between periods of autonomic response and brief moments of consciousness. The first sign of dawn appears, like a pink ribbon, over Arkansas cornfields in the east.

He tries to assemble the sequence of events that led him to this moment, but his mind is a river. Each time he reaches in with his hand, the memories fall through his fingers. He cannot hold anything still. Like an animal, he exists only for now.

The landscape entering and leaving the sphere of his lighted world is all he has. Cattails and fenceposts.

Lulu stirs and Jake turns to look at her. In that instant of inattention, he misses the night's only attempt at conversation. "Welcome to Louisiana," it says, by way of a sign at the side of the road. The state that bears his lover's name. A thought that will never occur to him. Not even with the aid of morning's clarity.

The Queen of the South. New Orleans. Both Lulu and Bobby are sleeping in the back seat, tucked into their dreams, when Jake floats down the left bank south of Pontchartrain into crescent city. They are sleeping still when he pulls off Clairborne onto Esplanade and draws up to a hotel on Chartres Street, where he books a room. A colonial, streetfront Creole façade with wrought-iron balconies draped in catalpas and ferns. It's the end of September and here the air is still thick with heat and humidity. People crowd a café across the street, spilling out onto a flowered patio, drinking iced coffee beneath the shade of a gazebo.

It is the racket of hoofbeats and a horse-drawn carriage on the granite-block street that finally awakens them.

"Oh, Jake. Tell me our room has a balcony," Lulu coos as she stretches languidly like a cat. Bobby doesn't speak at all. Instead, he stares dumbly up and down the street, entranced. As though he expects to see someone he knows.

"Why don't you and Bobby take the bag up to the room?" says Jake. "I'll go see if I can get tickets on the next boat to Cuba."

"Bring us something to eat on your way back," Lulu calls as

she bounds up the front steps, leaving Bobby to struggle with the bag. "Beignets," comes a disembodied voice.

Jake follows the hotelier's instructions to the Customs House. He elects to walk, after hours in the car, passing the Ursuline Convent with its unique brick gateway opening onto courtyard herb gardens. Jazz pours out of the alleys as he passes the wharves on his way to Decatur and the French Market—a twenty-four-hour bazaar jammed with hawkers and the hawked. Jake is jostled and accosted, but the river pulls him on, and soon he comes out onto Jackson Square, framed on either side by the Pontalba Buildings. The antique cathedral at the north end of the square looms over artists and jugglers. Supported by the crutches of Cabildo and the Presbytere. On his left, between him and the river, is Founders Park, its cannon pointed out over the square in an odd twist of history. From the levee, Jake watches a riverboat paddle upstream against the water's ancient flow. Algiers rises through a haze on the far shore.

At any other time, he might be awed by such a sight, the very thought of where he is right now. But the river only reminds him of Montreal, of how far away he is from where he thought to be. And the exhaustion doesn't help. Like observing the world through gauze. A filter of translucent glass that mutes even sound as it attempts to pass through.

He tries to imagine Israel now, to draw some satisfaction from his actions over the last few weeks, but even this doesn't work. His mind turns to Bobby in its wandering and he wonders, for the first time seriously, about the boy's involvement with Lulu. And her investment in him. At the risk of losing Lulu, he's said very little about the boy. Only now, Jake wants a fresh start. With or without the money. With or without the girl. He's had a long night to think about the situation. The way his life has spun out of his control since Lulu entered smiling. He has not had as long a night since J-P's death. And, in a similar way, he has been lost in the wilderness ever since. Fumbling through darkness. He imagined as a child that he understood what it was to live. But he has held on to that simplistic notion well into adulthood. J-P's sister understands better than he the meaning of life, what it means to get through each day—whether it bring sorrow or laughter—and then wake up to the next. This is all that is important, Jake realizes as he watches the riverboat struggle and a barge glide past in the opposite direction.

And even though he set out from the hotel intent on buying three passages to Cuba, he turns his back on the river and retraces his steps through the Latin Quarter with the heat of the late afternoon sun on his back. He will divide the money three ways, he thinks. And he will ask Lulu to come with him. Not to Cuba. He has more important plans for his share of the money now. But anywhere else, where he can find work and begin again.

The concierge recognizes Jake as he enters the lobby and passes him a key to the room. But even as Jake fits it into the ancient lock and listens for that familiar sliding, he is filled with a sense of foreboding. His senses lean into the room ahead of him, but all is dark. Sun bleeds red through the drawn shades. Beyond them is the balcony. Unable to locate the light switch, Jake crosses the floor.

He is not sure whether it is the movement or the sound of parted sheets that signals a presence there. His hand is almost on the blind when he senses it.

"Lulu?" The question is out before he turns to see them together. Just silhouettes before he lifts the sash and anchors them in the unforgiving light. Lulu's eyes oddly calm and cold, her head lifted only slightly from the pillow, arm across the sheets, guarding her chest. And the other woman caught in transition, naked and turning, eyes wide and white. One arm reaching, hovering outstretched.

"Bobby?" The realization hits Jake like a hammer in the centre of his chest. But the recognition, spoken aloud, eliminates the woman's uncertainty and her hand lands on the black handle. Turns it into a missile before his eyes. He's been here before.

Stumbling backward, Jake strikes out with his left hand, attempts to make contact with the door frame, to arrest his fall. But all the strength is gone from his fingers. When he looks at his chest, he is surprised to see a knife there. And a moment later, he is tipping away from the room. From Lulu. From Bobby.

Someone screams in the street below.

Knife and Thrower, 1927

It's not the thrower but the target that's important. This was the only piece of useful advice Bobby's father had ever provided her. So when she entered the almshouse for orphans at the age of twelve, she tested his theory on the other inmates. The easy boys in particular, the ones who followed her with their eyes, the ones who made it difficult to be a woman. Of course, kitchen knives weren't nearly as accurate as the balanced daggers of her father's profession. And she was sure to use this in her defence, after hitting—or missing—depending on her original intention. In the end, it was the matter of her uncertain intentions that finally convinced the boys to avert their eyes.

Bobby's father had been a knife thrower in the circus. Her mother, the first target. But the turnover in that profession is high. She left them outside Tucson several weeks before Bobby turned four.

A few drinks can steady a man's hands, but a few more will ruin them. And within a year, Bobby's father had been thrown out of every reputable touring circus in the southwest. When he was bingeing, Bobby was forced to take the case of finely honed knives into the streets. She juggled for pennies. Performance was bred into her. And when she was older, she often took her father's place on stage, a practice that alarmed each new target, but consoled those women desperate enough to stay on more than a few weeks. An occurrence that became increasingly rare. That is, until Joele.

Joele arrived from some hole in Louisiana, a sinking backwater in the delta. She was a mixture of French and Spanish, and possibly Negro—although it wasn't a fact she peddled to strangers. For whatever reason, she took it upon herself to save Bobby's father, and for that, Bobby loved her.

Joele could not have been more than sixteen, but she was escaping a whole other life that only came to Bobby in small bits and pieces like the shards of a broken mirror, the horror of which gave her an aura of wisdom beyond her years. And for a while, things were as they were before. Bobby's father was the Duke of Daggers again and he swore off drink for nearly a year.

Things might have turned out differently for Bobby and her father had Joele not fallen for a tightrope walker closer to her age. This made what happened next all the more suspect. The defence attorney argued that the Duke of Daggers had simply made an error, that the job of the target was inherently dangerous, and that one must expect accidents. But the prosecutor had witnesses lined up out the door, each of them with sworn testimony concerning an argument that took place before that evening's show. Miraculously, Joele recovered, but Bobby never saw her, or her father, again.

Four years she rotted in the almshouse, untouched and unmolested for the most part. But also friendless. She did not think about her father much, but for reasons unclear to her, Bobby often dreamed of Joele, of her cropped dark head and liquid mouth, of her waif-like frame and the press of her two small breasts when they embraced. Hot and shivering in the dark of the dorm room, she would wake in a pool of her own sweat.

And then one night she dreamed that Joele was holding her, rocking her back and forth on the cot where she used to sleep. The other woman held her so close, Bobby could hardly breathe. And even though she was consoled, she was frightened of something unidentifiable. And she could not—would not—stop crying, until the bed began to sink through the floor. Slowly at first. But eventually layers of earth flitted by like the picture shows. And all at once she was suffused by warmth. A tenderness she could only faintly remember from childhood—at her mother's breast. She awoke that night under the impression she had cried out, but the dorm was still. She remained that way—half asleep and half awake—for a long time. The sky washed slowly from black to blue and then to green. Eventually, the sun eked through the window as a grainy yellow light.

She understood something that morning she had always doubted in herself. And she knew she had to leave that place.

Of course, the only thing her father left her were the knives, so she took them when she escaped. Not for sentimental reasons, but because she had no money. It was the only thing of value that she owned, the only thing she was willing to trade.

On the night she chose to leave, Bobby cut her hair. Long, dark locks littered the bathroom floor about her feet. She did this because she had seen enough single women to understand that she didn't want to be one. The lonely schoolmistresses who passed in and out of the almshouse like ghosts. The washerwomen long past marrying age, with colourless hair and red, chapped hands. But when Bobby looked into the mirror above the sink, she saw Joele—her fierce spirit brewing like a storm.

The clothes were easy enough to come by. Boys of every age populated the orphanage. She borrowed pants from one, shoes from another. The process was nothing short of a metamorphosis. Even on the inside she felt changed. And when she placed the cap on her head, the transformation was complete. The shadow of its peak roughened the lines in her face, adding character.

Because the wards were locked at night, she spent a week filing through the bars of an upstairs window. She tossed the case of knives before her, then hung from the sill for a three-count. Just long enough to wish her roommates goodnight.

"Fuckers," she spit, and then dropped into the garden.

In the end, it was her hands that gave her away.

She had escaped cleanly, and found no trouble adopting the swagger she had observed in all the almshouse boys. The masquerade might have gone on forever had it not been for her hands. Bobby hitched and begged her way into Mississippi, en route to New Orleans, the only place she could imagine finding Joele. Outside Jackson, she found her first job on a road crew, digging a drainage ditch alongside a new government-sponsored highway. The pay was awful, but the employment allowed her to bed down and eat in the camp with the other men.

She studied the anatomy of their conversation around the harvest table and stole their speech like a parrot. She also absorbed their false bravado in the bunkhouse, their naked jostling as they paraded to and from the bathhouse, flesh swinging between their legs like trophies. But mostly, Bobby tried to stay out of their way. She was Gulliver in a world of giants.

But men search for weakness like water seeks the lowest point in a landscape. She had been the butt of jokes for a week, boorish jeers and insults. At sixteen, she made a small man. A boy, really. It was a struggle, in the beginning, to lift the pick-axe above her head. The first few days were hell. Her hands bled raw, open wounds until the palms were two big blisters. She tried binding them with rags, but they wore through and fell away by noon.

It was the pig they called Chub who discovered her. She had sneaked out to the woods to pee. She was exhausted. And even though he made more noise than a wild boar crashing through the brush, Bobby's senses were a mess. She did not pick him up until his hot breath was at her neck. She tried to scream, but his hand covered her mouth. She swallowed the dirt smell of it.

"Be quiet, kid," he whispered, though there was no need. "I bin up fer attempted murder. But if you play along, I'll be gentle as yer momma."

His fly was already open. The short, thick cock was pressed into the small of her back like a pistol. She struggled, but he had both her arms pinned to her sides. With his full weight upon her, they crashed forward into the leaves and the undergrowth of the forest floor. Her lungs collapsed under the pressure of the fall. She had not even had the time to button her own trousers before Chub arrived, and they were now helplessly about her ankles. Like a set of irons, they hindered any chance of escape.

He released her arms, secure in the knowledge that the bulk of his body now held her prisoner. Bobby's head was turned to the side. It was full of earth and loam. He kissed her with his slug-like tongue, probing her ear.

"The first time's always the worst, son. But if you scream, yer likely to attract more customers than help."

He did not know, then, she thought, amid the confusion.

"Come on, boy. It doesn't have to be this way. Show me them nice soft hands of yers. I got something you can hold."

Bobby tried one last time to roll the pig from her back, but he was much too heavy. And then the shock of his fingers between her legs stilled her. Bobby's eyes remained wide open, taking in the moss-covered trunks, the scrub brush of the forest floor. She held her breath. But the moment his hands came in contact with her, he too paused, and then withdrew as though burned.

"Jesus." The man rolled awkwardly off her back and scrambled to the nearest tree. He sat there on his ass, with his back against the trunk and his legs splayed out in front of him. His left boot almost touched her chin. He was breathing hard now, and when she looked up at him dumbly, Bobby could see the mushroom cap of his penis poking out the open flap of his pants.

She rose first to her hands and knees, unsure of whether she could stand. She did not wish to make any sudden movements, but she was afraid he would recover himself before she did. Slowly and deliberately, she regained her feet and pulled up the trousers. She fitted each button in each hole and then dusted the leaves and the soil from her clothes. The man did not move, except to turn his head away.

When she was through, Bobby looked down at her attacker. Suddenly calm, she wanted to remember everything about him, the sweat at his temples, his protruding belly, like an overripe pumpkin, and the shrunken, helpless penis, lost now in a mat of dark curly hair. After a minute, she turned in the direction of the work crew and walked away. The man did not pursue her.

In the days that followed, Bobby abandoned her quest for New Orleans and struck out for the circus. A place for freaks. And the only place she had ever felt at home.

She ran directly into the arms of The Guthrie Brothers Travelling Roadside Show and was taken on immediately as a juggler. Without a target, there was no other option. And without a reputation, there would never be a target for her knife-throwing act. She used rings and balls and bowling pins. She even experimented with flaming torches. But it was the knives to which she always returned. They called to her in her sleep. Twinkled like teeth each time she opened the case. And, of course, they carried the memory of Joele like a faded reflection in the blade.

Bobby kept the short hair, slicked it back like Valentino. That patent leather shine. And she bought new clothes with her first wages—fine black trousers and a milk white shirt. She thought it over and adopted a tie. The new duds added years to her appearance. On her evenings off, she wandered into dance halls, blind pigs, and speakeasies. No one suspected a thing. And she grew confident in her new anatomy. After a few weeks, she even began to smoke.

Francis, the eldest of the Guthrie brothers, was happy with Bobby's work. The show was popular. She could keep six daggers twirling above her head and was working on another. Her goal was to have all eight knives from her case spinning like propellers. Between the damage she incurred on the road crew, and the myriad of nicks and cuts she received from the blades, Bobby's hands were catching up with her new self. They would never betray her again.

Sometimes, she took a drink with the trapeze artists, or tagged along with the road crew. But mostly, she spent her time alone. The circus was slowly wending north to the east coast—last stop Coney Island, where they would stay for the summer season. And Bobby was practising daily. This was not the life she imagined for herself, but she was dreaming of Joele more and more. And the dreams disturbed her. Again and again she found herself awakened with that same warm infusion, the rush of a knife released. But it only left her lonely and unable to return to sleep. However, the constant practise wore her down, so that she was exhausted and ready to collapse in the act of juggling. She kept her eye on the blades. Always spinning, twisting upward and away. Always returning, falling into the palm of her waiting hand. The act was like a test of faith, but no matter how often the knives slipped away, she was surprised by the cold steel of the blade. The warm release of each new wound.

Lulu appeared to her, the first time, through a thin veil of smoke. The circus was stopped in Wheeling, West Virginia. They arrived late and left off setting up until morning. Bobby, tired but still unable to bed down, spent her pocket money on a ticket to the Grand Theatre. The billing for Oswald Williams promised magic and coin tricks. But the man on the poster bore little resemblance to the elderly magician scurrying about on stage. The performance was lacklustre and the audience was worse. Williams depended heavily on mechanical illusions, but his work with the cabinet was transparent, even to Bobby, who was unfamiliar with the genre. And, as if to make up for it, he ended each trick with same poor puff of smoke, so that by the halfway mark of the show, the air was thick with the stuff and the less patient patrons had already begun to leave.

But it was Lulu, his lovely assistant, who kept Bobby in her seat. She appeared from the inside of the cabinet early in the performance, the supposed transformation of a small, white rabbit, placed inside only moments before. Complete with whiskers, bunny ears, and a tail fashioned from cotton, she stepped through a whiff of smoke and into the gaze of a piti-less crowd. Through it all, she smiled and modelled in the wake of the floodlights. She encouraged what meagre applause she could by clapping herself. And all the while, Bobby fol-lowed her every move, entranced by the quiet suffering and by what she misconstrued as stoic composure—the counterpart of silent desperation.

Bobby waited in the shadows outside the theatre. She could hardly believe herself, the daring of what she was about to attempt. The sheer recklessness. It was the same sensation—distant but not forgotten—that she used to experience while throwing her father's knives. It was strange, she thought, how foreign that little girl was to her now. A ragged doll with long, straight hair and a faded dress, trembling before the small audi-ence, reducing the crowd in her mind to a pinprick in her con-sciousness, the way her father explained it to her once, through a blur of drink. Erasing them, so that only the target remained.

And then cradling that target like a hurt bird, cupping its life in her hands one last time, before tossing the blade. The cool thwack of its landing swallowed up in the breath of the crowd.

As Bobby remembered, Lulu stepped through the front doors of the Grand Theatre and out onto the sidewalk. She wore a light coat over a loose-fitting dress. A small emerald hat covered her head. It was dark, but warm. The day's heat still trapped in the earth. The little magician was not far behind, still sporting his tuxedo, but he only spoke to her in parting, and signalled a cab. The woman turned when he was gone and set off purposefully in the opposite direction. Bobby left the safety of her doorway and crossed the traffic in pursuit. She was not clear in her mind what it was she hoped to achieve, whether she would be content just to follow her, or whether she would attempt something more dangerous. Bobby was not quite sure why she was there to begin with. What drew her to this woman? Perhaps it was her resemblance to Joele, she thought. Physically, they were very different. Lulu was tall and broad-shouldered. Her hair was unfashionably long. But there were other similarities, like the suggestion of a past.

Around the corner from the theatre, there was a movie house. Lulu paid for a ticket and entered. The film had already begun when Bobby arrived. It may have been past the first intermission, from what she could gather on the screen. At first, she could see very little, other than Douglas Fairbanks and Mary Pickford, leaning in to one another. But when her eyes adjusted to the low lighting, she realized that Lulu had not taken a seat. She was, in fact, standing at the back of the room, only a few steps from Bobby. The unexpected proximity caused her to catch her breath. The woman turned in response, and for a moment their eyes met.

"I know it seems odd to be arriving so late," she whispered to Bobby. "But I've seen it twice already."

Bobby had not expected to be drawn into the woman's world so immediately. And the best answer she could think of was a lie. "Yes, me too."

Lulu's smile was an invitation to conspire.

As they were leaving the movie house, she said to Bobby, "You followed me here."

And all her efforts to be suave and debonaire during the film were pulled like a tablecloth, scattering dishes and utensils in a clatter of noise.

"I saw you waiting across the street from the Grand," the woman continued. "Oh, don't worry. I'm not frightened. Not of you. Did you see the show?"

Bobby thought initially to deny Lulu's presumption, but she couldn't find the opportunity to fit a word in and now it seemed redundant.

"Yes," she said. "I was in the second row."

"So you admit it, then!" Lulu exclaimed. And Bobby could not help but blush.

"Oh, don't be shy. I'm being rather forward, aren't I? And you're awfully young. How old are you? Never mind. Buy me a drink."

Bobby opened her mouth to respond, but could not answer.

"I know a place we can go," Lulu added. "Will you take me?"

"Lead on," Bobby said, regaining her composure, or at least the semblance of composure. Inside, her heart was racing.

When they entered the haze of the club, the jazz band was playing "Birth of the Blues." It was a converted cellar, really, with a boiler in the far corner. The ceilings were low. Bobby's swagger had returned. Her voice was settled. This was farther than she had ever carried the charade and she was curious to know if she could pull it off.

Fortunately, Lulu did most of the talking. She admitted to the show's failure and to Williams' incompetence.

"I'm hoping to be discovered by vaudeville, and then maybe the pictures," she said. "Don't you think I look a little like Mary Pickford?" Lulu talked about everything and nothing all at once. She was guarded and careful about her past, but expansive about her aspirations and her prospects.

Bobby tried her best to seem tough and at ease with women. She smoked to occupy her hands, but the longer she was in Lulu's company, the more difficult it was to remain aloof. She recognized the feeling in her stomach as the same one she experienced in her dreams of Joele. And at that moment, she had never understood better what that sensation meant for her. And because of that, no matter how close she sat to Lulu, there seemed to be an unbridgeable gap between them, yawning like a mouth. The band was playing "Let's Do it, Let's Fall in Love," and several couples moved about the makeshift dance floor in time to the music. Bobby could feel the moment slipping away and, try as she might, she was unable to reduce the room. The woman she had made her target blurred and bent. And just then, as though Lulu could sense it too, she leaned in to kiss her. It was what Bobby wanted to happen then more than anything, but she couldn't seem to let it happen, and, at the last moment, she pulled back from Lulu's advance. She fumbled for something to say as an excuse, only the woman stopped her. Placed her painted finger against Bobby's lips.

"I know," she said. "I know."

Somehow, Bobby believed her. And when Lulu leaned in a second time, Bobby made no effort to stop her. Not since Joele had another person touched her with such tenderness. And Bobby knew immediately, it was exactly what she had been searching for.

Only a short walk from the circus grounds, there was a barn. Swallows flitted in the rafters. As the women entered, a lonely pigeon burst upward like a startled heart. Otherwise, it was a quiet place, falling into ruin. Its split sides caught the first rays of morning sunlight like vertical blinds, tattooing the floor with their shadows. Dust and chaff hung in the white motes. Yes, this is right, Bobby thought. This is perfect. The palm of Lulu's hand was intertwined with her own, clammy with heat and perspiration. In her right hand, Bobby carried a battered case.

She turned on the other woman and kissed her again, as she had so many times through the night. And yet, each time was a surprise. The shock of a dropped blade. Now that she had been discovered—revealed and accepted—Bobby experienced a new sense of self, of belonging to the world. And she could not resist testing her new body, her sexual self. The one who loved a beautiful woman. The one who was loved. But as wondrous as that new rush was, she could not help but think that there must be more. Each kiss ended in a disappointment. She wished to draw the woman closer, to possess her. And yet something told her that this would never be entirely possible.

"What are we doing here?" Lulu asked, their faces only inches apart. "When will you tell me what is in the case?"

"Do you trust me, Lulu?" It was an unfair question, and she knew it. She made the same propietary demands of Joele. But she felt that she must have this. All love, no matter how fresh, was a leap of faith.

After an almost imperceptible hesitation, Lulu nodded.

Bobby led her to one end of the barn and pressed her back against the grain of the wood. The sun had risen higher since their arrival and the tentacles of light crawled over the woman's body. To her, Bobby must have appeared like a partial eclipse. She arranged Lulu's arms out to either side—so that she took on the form of a cross—and then stepped backward twenty paces to the case of knives.

The first shot entered the barnboards a full foot above Lulu's left arm. She could not see it coming in the light. Its sharp announcement caused her to suck wind through her teeth, but she did not scream.

"Don't move," Bobby warned, and the second and third daggers punctured the wall under her right shoulder, the inside left knee.

The barn was shrinking, reducing itself to a tunnel of air between thrower and target. Bobby's knives sang along that shaft, crashed harmless as raindrops around the woman's head. Lulu closed her eyes, the final act of faith, of giving. And to Bobby, the next two daggers were more binding than a marriage. The last one struck home between the ring and middle fingers of Lulu's left hand. She had found her target. A tiny rivulet of blood formed the band.

THE SHADOW, 1930

Jake dreams about water. About death. He is just beneath the surface of a lake. He is on his back, looking up at light, diffuse and shifting, amorphous through waves. He cannot breathe, but this does not seem important. There is no sound and he is perfectly still. He could not move if he wanted. The water is neither warm nor cool, and he is not sure that it is wet, or that he is frightened.

Somewhere on the edge of his consciousness, Jake realizes that this is a dream. And this is a safe thought, as he does not know to what he will awaken. But naming the dream is enough to end it, and soon he is fighting, thrashing like a fish against the body's urge to surface.

Only as he breaks the waves does his body cry out for air, and he awakens gasping from his hospital bed, reeling in the foreign surroundings of an all-white room. He is not sure what he expected, not sure he even understands in a conscious way how it is he arrived here, or where here is. It is the most incongruous part of his awakening that brings it all back to him. Lulu and Bobby. The hotel in New Orleans. The knife. It is the presence of Israel sitting quietly with his legs crossed in a chair at the end of his bed that causes the memories to tumble in upon him. And as he squints, growing quickly accustomed to the light, Jake realizes that Benji is also there, guarding the door like an ancient stone sentinel.

Only as his situation sinks in does Jake recognize the pain in his chest, his arm in a sling. He lies back into the cushioned haven of his bed and closes his eyes.

"You're awake," says Israel flatly, belying no sense of the man's emotional state. Though Jake can only guess. "Benji thinks we should kill you."

Jake opens his eyes. "You expect me to believe he thinks." Jake imagines that he sees the ghost of a ripple run through the flunkie's face. No more.

"Don't make matters worse, *boyo*. For your father's sake."

"Fuck him," Jake manages, feeling a general weakness settle over him like a cat on his chest. "Fuck you."

Israel ignores the outburst completely. That's what Jake remembers about him, the poise.

"You've had quite an accident, son. Do not upset yourself."

Jake struggles to say something else but he can't manage enough air, and it comes out as a sigh.

"I would, you know . . . kill you, that is," Israel continues. "You put me in a very awkward position, after all. And my creditors have a particularly nasty way of collecting, shall we say."

Jake can do nothing but listen, but he pictures Israel and Benji cut down in a hail of bullets, just like the Valentine's Day Massacre the year before. Not at all a disagreeable image, he thinks.

"But I think to myself, Jacob. I think to myself that we are kindred spirits in this. You and I."

Jake reopens his eyes, stares fixedly at the wavering vision of the man in white. Older now, he thinks. Older even than he was days ago.

"You see, we are both patsies here. We have both lost something of value."

"Lulu," Jake says softly and then looks away, ashamed almost to admit that it is a loss, even now.

"Louisa. Yes," answers Israel. "A complicated woman. Many different names. Different faces. What was she to you, Jacob?"

The question, surely meant to be rhetorical, makes Jake consider. Life raft. Ruin. Those and many others, at the very least.

"The worst part of this, Jacob, is that I knew about the boy all along. I met him on Coney Island. I saw him tossing daggers. I could have rubbed him out at any time. But I didn't. For Louisa's sake. Who is he, Jacob? Tell me this." Israel's anger surfaces for the first time. He leans forward, face gone red as a burn. "Nothing," he says, using his hands to illustrate the insignificance. "Nothing." Israel's voice returns to its calm, reflective drawl with the last word, and then he leans back in his chair, recrosses his legs.

Him, Jake thinks. *He*. Israel does not know Bobby at all. One card he will hold back, for the time being.

"I need that money, Jacob." Israel picks lint off the sleeve of his jacket and tosses it onto the floor. "I know you can get it back. Am I right?"

Jake tries to hold the man's gaze and fails.

"There is a gun in your night table. An envelope with money. Enough, I think." Israel is standing now. Benji's hand is on the door. "You get this money for me, Jacob. You get it and all is forgiven."

Israel leaves the room without another word. Benji follows, stopping only long enough to shake his head and produce some semblance of a chuckle.

Jake resists the urge to check his night stand until the men's footsteps have disappeared from the hallway. Then, with his good left hand, he reaches over to withdraw the tiny drawer. The pain, not as acute as it was earlier, is still there. He remembers very little about the fall, but miraculously it does not seem to have injured him seriously. His collarbone, he suspects, has been dislocated. But otherwise he is fine. The wound where the knife entered does not appear to have penetrated his chest. Glanced off a rib, perhaps. Superficial. The biggest problem, then, is the concussion. For surely the rush of vertigo as he bends forward is a result of head trauma.

A small nine-millimetre Luger rests in the drawer, its dark potential gleaming. He withdraws the envelope and sits back, fighting the urge to vomit. When the feeling passes, he flicks through the series of bills within. Five hundred dollars and a glamour shot of Lulu. Israel is serious, he thinks.

For days after the accident, Bobby mopes about their new palatial home, afraid that she will run across Jake in the street. Perhaps even more frightened that she will not. The hotel has effected an admirable hush job. Not a word appears in any of the local papers. Murder is bad for business, she thinks. A little money to grease the wheels, and . . . New Orleans is a big city.

Lulu feigns oblivion, comes and goes as she pleases, returns always with an armload of boxes. Dresses and hats, shoes for every gown. And there is always something for Bobby. A new comb the last time—whalebone inlaid with mother-of-pearl. Now that her hair is down and too short for styling, something has to be done, or so Lulu professes.

It has been years since Bobby wore a dress, and she finds herself tugging at it constantly, shifting in the awkward garment. Bare knees make her feel naked.

It was her idea to come to New Orleans, but Lulu is in love with the city and their new home. Windows and doors are thrown open to air, the scent of clematis. Crêpe myrtle.

Bobby feels almost silly to have come at all—an adult who realizes too late that fairy tales do not come true. Though she has little choice but to forge onward now that she is here, descend into the city to search for shadows that may not be partial to discovery. Or that may not have even passed this way at all.

Cuba is a red herring Jake is not about to swallow. He is released from the hospital into the streets of New Orleans within a week. Israel picks up the tab. Jake has not seen the man or his flunkie since he first awakened after the fall. But he isn't convinced that the man has left New Orleans, either. It's a good town to hide out in.

His arm is still weak, his head only slightly muddled. As long as Jake remains upright, the pain is insubstantial. The entry wound from Bobby's knife has left a small, puckered mark above his heart, like a kiss. Two red lips.

He carries the gun in his pocket. The envelope in his pants.

This is how he enters the world after days of inactivity, dishevelled and slow. Loping dangerously through a haunted city, looking for ghosts. Perhaps even pursued by a few. As he lay in the hospital bed, considering Israel's request, Jake decided he was not angry enough to use the pistol on Lulu or Bobby. But he does want answers. And money. Not for Israel, though. Jake will face the mobster later, when the time comes. But for now, he has afforded Jake the means to track down the women. And Jake intends to do just that. New Orleans was not a random destination chosen on a whim, as Lulu would have him believe. If his instincts are right, and he does have serious reason to doubt them of late, then the women are still here.

During his first few days of freedom, Jake descends into the Vieux Carré, takes a room on Toulouse, and slides from jazz bar to jazz bar, buying illegal drinks for the regulars and passing Lulu's photo around. He is awed by the decadence and seduced by the music. Jake catches the musician Nick Larocca at an underground speakeasy on Bourbon. New Orleans is a town that blooms at night like a luminescent flower—a city of Jekyll and Hyde. The Old Absinthe House, the Maison Bourbon. Eventually, Jake crawls through every back-alley dive in the Quarter, his head reeling with jazz licks and black women. Chartres is a tunnel beneath cobwebs of streetcar cable. Royal, a lesson in Creole ironwork.

Friday afternoon Jake stumbles into a fat Negro in a three-piece suit. A swath of red material cuts through his corpulent mass like the sash of a pageant contestant. He lumbers rhythmic at the head of a dark parade, top hat and monocle. His body is a bowling pin. The music that swims over Jake only after the encounter tells him that he is now part of a funeral march—an age-old African tradition set to New Orleans jazz. The band, loosely strung out among the mourners, plays "Free as a Bird," slow and simple. The clatter of the horse-drawn carriage—the hearse where the body lies—seems to be a part of the tune.

Some of the women in the march carry black umbrellas. Others mop their eyes with handkerchiefs. Without thinking,

Jake turns and walks with them, hovering on the outside of their party as they roll down Conti, where the players switch to "Nearer My God to Thee."

Jake adopts the crowd's steady sway, leans into the music.

At the cemetery on Basin, a man with a snare drum hammers out a kind of taps as they lower the body into the ground, and then everything changes. The band launches into an up-tempo version of "Didn't He Ramble," and leads the mourners like a Pied Piper back out into the streets.

That night, Jake takes a cab to the Orpheum Theatre, not because he expects to find the girls there, but because he has been drinking since noon, and by nine o'clock he is full of self-loathing. He fools himself into thinking otherwise. However, an evening at the Orpheum is like holding a mirror up to the way things might have been. It's a punishment. His way of earning indulgence.

He is unable to sit through the show.

Imro Fox is a well-known magician, but he has never been a big noise on the vaudeville circuit. In essence, he's a hack and Jake sees right through the performer's comic stylings as a means of masking his deficiencies as an illusionist. But what really frustrates Jake is the audience's forgiveness. The man's entire act is an apology.

During a particularly poor staging of the Metamorphosis, Jake calls out, "He's behind the curtain!"

The outburst is picked up only by those immediately in his vicinity, but they do their best to ignore the unshaven mess of him. The tacit acceptance only goads him on, however, and his heckling grows more intrusive. He scoffs openly and laughs at the most inopportune moments, even calls out the punchlines to bad jokes.

Jake's only disappointment when he is thrown out is that it didn't happen sooner.

Drunk and exasperated with his failure, he stumbles into a clapboard shack on Front Street, a violent hole by the harbour with a smoking trumpet on stage. Jake draws more than a few glances from the predominantly coloured crowd, but no one bothers him. After a while, he notices a Creole girl holding up the other end of the bar—a small, dark-skinned woman, possibly mulatto, with short, bobbed hair and a ruined face. A scar runs from the cradle of her left eye clear down to the edge of her lip in the form of a sickle. She slinks around the counter in a knee-length dress and bare feet, heading straight for Jake. That's when he realizes what she is.

"You shouldn't be here, sugar," she purrs in a voice to match the face. "Let me take you home."

"Actually, I'm looking for someone," he says, reaching into his jacket for the photograph. "Maybe you've seen her around." The edges of the picture are soiled and curled from excessive handling, but the likeness is fine.

The woman's face changes as she takes the image into her hands.

"Where'd you get this?" she asks.

"You know her?" Jake's mind tries desperately to surface from the drink.

"I wouldn't say that. She's the acquaintance of an old friend." The woman's face softens, though.

"Bobby," Jake says, and her face looks up into his, searching him for possible motive.

"Yeah," she says simply, nodding her head. "Who are you?"

"Jake."

"You ain't no mobster," she says as though he's been caught in a lie.

"No," he says.

A big man further along the bar is giving them the eye.

"We'd better get outa here, sugar," she intones, leading him by the sleeve.

On their way out, Jake asks her, "Who are you?"

"Around here they call me Miss Josephine," she answers as they reach the door. "But you can call me Joele." The trumpet breaks into "Sweet Georgia Brown."

Death.

Houdini had a fascination with it. Made midnight trips to local graveyards, toured the world's finest cemeteries. Montmartre. Père Lachaise. St. Marx. Sometimes he brought charcoal and onionskin, gathered the inscriptions of great men and women like others collected stamps. His fingers grew dark with the residue. The tongue in his mouth traced the lines, his brow furrowed and bent to the task.

Know thy enemy, he thought. Familiarize yourself with his mannerisms, his habits. For Houdini, the enemy was never far away. That's the way he liked it. Life as a high-wire act, thinking nothing but edge, so that when death arrived—as welcome as an unwanted salesman—he might choose to jump instead. And never lose the element of surprise.

After a lifetime of covering her tracks, Joele tells Jake everything, even the things he doesn't need to know. The names of lost lovers. A good recipe for preparing catfish. She watches him drift in and out of sleep as she allows her story to wander and then pulls it back like a kite on the wind. But she never doubts that he is listening. He does not try to stop her or direct her in any one direction. He simply soaks it all in like the shore does the tide, allowing the immaterial information to flow back out to sea. Keeping the smooth stones.

"They called him the Duke of Daggers," she tells him and laughs. "He was one pretentious sonofabitch. But he could afford to be. I knew I'd like him from the start. And there's something to be said about a target."

Joele pauses then. She has finally come to the part he is searching for. Jake's body belies any change in attitude, any sharpening of the senses. He remains slouched in the chair by the window, a hunchback silhouette, waiting patiently, letting the story unfold.

And so she begins again.

Joele speaks to him of Bobby's childhood, talks of knives into the night, and falls asleep in the warm bath of his bed. Leaving Jake alone at dawn and imagining the circus, the freaks and the buffoons. How much he has in common with people on the margin. The woman is a seahorse curled into the white sheets, dreaming. She is not so old as he first believed. Her back is still a river, the taut current of an acrobat, bronze depths and eddies. A figment of the Mississippi. But her face conveys a different story. She is the spirit of New Orleans.

But then again, he thinks, we are all a jumble of conflicting tales, the contents of a hastily packed suitcase. What does he really know of Bobby? Even now, just pieces. Jake has barely scratched the surface with Lulu. And perhaps he must content himself with that, reconcile himself to the measurement of a half-life, or none at all. He could turn now and walk away. But not really. That would not be living.

He has found them, thanks to Joele. It was they who sought her out. Bobby was afraid, Joele claimed, or maybe just confused. Joele did not trust Lulu and she told the girl as much. Lulu wore danger like a perfume, she said. She'd seen her type before. But the girls had gone uptown, come into money. Bobby wanted to help, but Joele turned her down, told her to take that money and escape. That Lulu was bad news. But Bobby left her new address behind. They'd gone across Canal to the Garden District, upstream from Jackson Avenue and on the riverside of St. Charles. Prytania St. on the corner of First. A fully furnished rental, Joele told him. Top hat. *I want to spend my money in New Orleans*, Jake thinks.

He is light-headed with days of insomnia and drink. He retrieves the gun beneath the mattress, beneath Joele, and counts the remaining cash before replacing the envelope deep in his pants. Just because she will not take money from Bobby does not mean that she would be adverse to taking his. Then Jake closes his eyes for the first time since his release. It will give the woman a chance to leave before he awakens.

She can smell the men on Lulu's clothes, their hands in her hair. Somewhere inside, Bobby has known all along that it would never end. Not even after they hit the jackpot. But denial is a powerful drug. Lulu's chest rises and falls beneath the single cotton sheet like a pale blue heartbeat in the light of the waxing moon. Sleep comes easily to those without conscience.

Bobby is curled into the windowsill of the upstairs dormer, legs crossed, knees pulled almost to her chin. The window is open, but no one is about in this part of the city. Her naked glow unseen by prying eyes. She blows smoke rings from one of Lulu's cigarettes.

Joele is an injured animal, she thinks, misused and much abused in the years since her departure. It was not the reunion she expected, but then, how could it have been? Joele was not the only person changed. And Lulu only made it worse, hovering like a proprietary lover. When the woman told her to escape, Bobby begged her to come along. But she knew even as she pleaded that Joele would not acquiesce and that she herself could never leave, either. Both of them are locked in different orbits, and neither with enough volition left to kick off into the unknown. Their worlds, though dangerous, are mapped already, and therefore safe enough to navigate.

Bobby continues to blow smoke rings like wishes over the lawn as she stares off into the half-light of another approaching dawn.

Jake hops the streetcar named "Desire" as it groans up St. Charles and debarks at Lee Circle, beneath the white sculpture of the general. His walk down First is an education in affluence. Arthritic, live oak trees line the walk with a canopy of shadow. Palms compete with dogwood. Azaleas in full bloom. The gardens are just as old as the houses. Greek revival cottages from the era of Jefferson Davies. Antebellum excess and Victorian gingerbread. This is the wealth that slavery built—not unlike Westmount, its northern cousin raised on the backs of poor French and Irish and a dozen other immigrant classes.

It is late afternoon when he rounds Prytania, careful to stay out of view. The rented home is among the more ostentatious from the outside, set back from the street and hemmed in by ornate cast-iron fencing on stone walls. The garden is spare in comparison, consisting of live oak, Spanish moss, and a grove of crêpe myrtle, thick with pink blooms.

Jake is tempted just to walk in, but he made a plan while Joele slept through the morning, and it is the only thing that is important to him now. So instead, he watches from the shadow of an oak, lost under the baroque tangle of its prehistoric boughs. And eventually, his patience is rewarded.

A cab clatters to a heated stop outside the gate, its horn an intrusive blast that scatters the neighbourhood birds. Bobby leaves the doorway of the house first, her dark hair too short to be attractive, but loose about her ears like it was the morning she tried to kill him. Her small face almost childlike in its loveliness. White frock over olive skin. She is unrecognizable but for her worried eyes. And Lulu, like a long willow branch, follows after her.

She wears danger like a perfume.

Jake rests his head against the skin of the oak until he hears the cab rattle off in the direction of Canal. And then, like a thief, he steals across the quiet thoroughfare and through the front gate. Time is of the essence now.

Israel Karpowicz sits in the back seat of a cream-coloured Bentley. It is hardly the sort of vehicle one would use on a stakeout, but here in the Garden District of New Orleans, it is only another piece of the scenery, an extra stroke of the artist's brush in an already lush canvas. But even in the plush comfort of the automobile's red leather interior, the mobster is beset by demons. He can feel them circling like sharks at the scent of his blood. If he opens the door, they will rend him to pieces. He uses a silk handkerchief the colour of his suit to mop the perspiration beading on his brow.

Jacob entered the palatial home across the street almost fifteen minutes ago, only seconds after Lulu vacated the premises. The sight of her caused the old man's heart to skip. And for a moment he forgot that he was angry with her. That she had taken everything he had left, including his self-respect. Had she lingered even a moment beneath the shade of the live oak trees outside the home she bought with his money, he might have gone to her, forgiving everything. Her hold on him had always been such. But she did not linger. She didn't have it in her. She moved like a river instead, down the front steps and into the waiting car. And then she was gone. Israel hadn't even thought about the young woman at her side. She was superfluous.

"You want I should follow 'dem, boss?" Benji's ancient growl came to him like the hum of a distant saw. He sat like a barnacle in the driver's seat.

"No," Israel replied as Jacob slid across the street from his hiding place, a cat stealing into an abandoned chair. "We wait here." The mobster's resolution had returned.

Now, as he tarries in the late afternoon heat, he has only his thoughts to keep him company. Even as part of the man holds out for a miracle—the possibility of a comeback—Israel Karpowicz, the street Jew from Montreal, understands somewhere deep inside that the ride has come to an abrupt end. After years of scratching an existence out of that city's back alleys, of fighting his way into its rackets and intrigues, to a point where he finally commanded a modicum of respect, he finds the carpet ripped from under him like a cheap magic trick. His slow rise through the ranks of the criminal hierarchy is a mockery in comparison to the celerity of his collapse.

Where did it all go, he finds himself wondering—his mind slipping away from him, when he should be focussed on raking it all back. He had grown so used to the consolations of his wealth that he failed to understand the gravity of its disappearance. The St. Tropez had always bled money, but he didn't give it a second thought. Israel was awash in money from his illegal liquor trade. He let everything else slide because of it. He became a monoculture, a cash-cropper. But when the booze dried up, overnight the taps shut off. It was his failure to diversify. He was in love with the trappings of his own success. He surrounded himself with sycophants, women, and music. Unfortunately, parasites never stick with a dead host. And now he's alone again, with Benji, the way it used to be when they were kids. And, just as it was back then, the sharks are circling. Oddly, he didn't seem to notice them as a young man.

As his mind slides backward, searching for answers, Israel fails to notice Jacob as he leaves the house in a hurry, slipping down a side stair and out through the backyard.

It wasn't supposed to end like this, he thinks. But Israel has always been a fighter, an admirer of the underdog. The truth he avoids acknowledging is that he never bet on one.

Jake is seated in a wingbacked chair in the parlour of Lulu's new home when Bobby first sees him. He has returned just in time from his errand downtown. He imagines that to her he must appear like a ghost, inconsistent with the room's colonial decor, at the very least. The expression on her face confirms as much. But he is surprised to find relief there too, a sigh and a visible loosening of the muscles that hold her shoulders together.

"You're alive," she says, and then notices the gun in his hand like a toy. "How did you find us?"

"I met a friend of yours. Where's Lulu?"

"You don't need the gun. It was never in our plan to kill you."

"That's comforting."

"I panicked."

After years of hiding, Jake thinks, and he believes her. "Nonetheless. I'd rather not take any chances this time. Where's Lulu?" he asks again. And then continues, "Another man?"

"A man with a boat. On the lake," Bobby offers by way of explanation.

"Joele's worried about you."

"She only wants to see the lake." The girl ignores his comment, but her voice is small and unconvincing. "She'll be home soon."

"I'll wait," says Jake. "Have a seat."

Bobby chooses a chair across the room, beside a wall table where the previous occupants probably stacked their mail. It is bare now, and unlikely to ever be full under Lulu's occupation.

"What do you want?" she asks. "With us."

Jake cannot remain aloof. The truth is he isn't really sure what he wants. Everything he ever dreamt of is gone now.

Lulu is all he has left. He can't say that he only wants to ask her why. Or can he? Isn't Bobby just another victim like him?

"She couldn't tell you," says Bobby, as though she has read his thoughts. "It's just something she does."

Jake remembers that night long ago in Westmount, the young girl with the milk. Quietly chatting. *You should leave*, she told him.

The room is filled with shadows now, both real and imaginary. It is hard to tell the difference between them anymore, Jake thinks.

"So why are you still here?" he says.

"She's not through with me yet."

"Who is she, anyway?" Jake asks, and the question seems to take the girl by surprise. Bobby tilts her head and looks out the window filtered by sheers.

"I guess I don't really know. I thought I did once."

Jake is suddenly hungry for details.

"She's from the Midwest somewhere. Minnesota, maybe, if you can believe that. She doesn't exactly open up about that sort of thing, as you can imagine."

"Does she have any family?" Jake is not sure why he asks these questions. Perhaps he would like to understand the woman's motivations. But what is more likely is that he'd like to know about Lulu's other victims. How many lives has she pulled apart?

"Her parents are alive, I think. And she once mentioned a brother. But what does it matter, anyway?" she asks.

Jake cannot find the words to tell her.

But just then Lulu arrives in the room and everything changes. Neither Jake nor Bobby heard her enter the house. Her face is a mask. If she is surprised to see Jake, she does not show it. But she is not alone. Israel is behind, and Benji. Both men carry pistols waist-high as they enter the room. He has made so many errors, thinks Jake.

"This is like a reunion. Am I right?" says Israel. "Maybe Benji could fix us a cocktail?"

"Are you all right, Lulu?" asks Bobby, standing.

"Shut up," barks Israel in an uncharacteristic snarl. A strand of his slick hair has worked itself free and dangles chaotic over his brow. His clothes are not pressed.

He's on the run, thinks Jake. Desperate.

"Will somebody tell me who is this?" Israel scans the room for a response. He is quickly losing his cool.

"Bobby," says Jake. And the man squints as if to better comprehend. "The boy?" he asks, incredulous.

"Not exactly," responds Jake.

"You know what? I don't care. Give me the money you stole," Israel says, looking back and forth between the two women. When no one moves or speaks, he turns to Benji. "Kill the girl."

Somehow, Jake notices for the first time the letter opener on the table by Bobby's hand. Its insidious promise clear as the immediate future. Jake stands. "Bobby!"

But it is Israel who turns in response, the girl already in motion, reaching for the letter opener, a knife to her practised hand. "Drop the gun, Jake," he says, and then he careens backward past Benji, who turns his own head like a mechanical puppet. Israel's mouth is the shape of a plum. His body dead where it falls.

When Benji's gaze returns to the room, he levels the pistol at the thrower, who is lit by the last light of day, practically glowing.

Jake has no choice but to shoot him.

Bobby steals the keys to Israel's car from the pockets of a dead man and pulls it around onto Prytania. She has become a boy again, but Jake finds the disguise ridiculous now that he knows the truth. He can't understand how he ever missed it, though he's sure Lulu's distraction helped. He rummages through the cellar of the old house and comes up with several old coal bags. In the stables out back, he gathers up a length of rusty chain, an archaic lever action lock the size of his heart, horse-shoes, anything of weight that can be attached to the bodies.

He is shocked at the rapidity and the lucidity of Lulu's plan—its cold, diabolical effectiveness. It could be that she was out on the lake earlier and that the idea was close at hand, but Jake doubts that interpretation. He fears that she would have arrived at something equally Machiavellian under any other circumstances.

When he returns to the sitting room, she has already bound the bodies in expensive Turkish carpets. Bobby is waiting in a vehicle outside.

Lulu grasps at Israel's feet as though she were moving fur-niture, and Jake bends to pick up the head. It is a rough nego-tiation to get him out the main entrance, through the garden, and into the automobile, but eventually they succeed and return for the heavier mass that was Benji. Jake cannot lie to himself. He had imagined Benji's death on numerous occa-sions, contemplated the man's demise at his own hands, even. But he is far from satisfied now as he stumbles backward over the threshold of the parlour and into the vestibule, cradling the big man's ugly mug. Lulu can only push the feet, lifting them every now and then to clear a step or the edge of a rug.

To think that he had come here to salvage something of her seems ludicrous now. As he watches the woman struggling down the front steps, dishevelled and focussed, peering left and right to check the street, Jake cannot even venture what it was he had hoped to salvage. But he understands in some oblique way that she is like a mirror. Only, rather than a likeness, she reflects a yearning.

She is what you want her to be, and is therefore perfect.

Bobby drives the car without ceremony past the cemeteries south of Claiborne. In a town that parades its dead, their passage is unobtrusive. The silent tombs breathe out reproach, Jake thinks. The car wings on and eventually turns north toward the lake, flat as a prairie without end. Pontchartrain.

The marina is abandoned. The boats bob against their moorings, water laps about the pier. The few cypress trees bordering this area of the lake are festooned in garlands of Spanish moss. This time, the feet are left to Bobby as Lulu leads them out to a sleek powerboat. Its wooden hull gleams in the wet air of a waning moon. They lay Israel's body between the seats and Lulu stands guard over it, while Jake and Bobby trundle back to the car.

When they return with Benji, Lulu breaks the silence that has accompanied them since they left the Garden District.

"We'll drive them out several miles and dump the bodies in the middle of the lake," she says.

"And how will we find our way back in the dark?" asks Jake.

"We'll follow the lights of New Orleans. You can see for miles out there. The city looks like an island during the day."

It is Bobby who starts the boat and then emerges from beneath the console so that Lulu can captain them out into the lake. The drone from the engine discourages any further conversation, but Jake stares at Bobby the whole way, and she pretends not to notice. The wind disturbs the patent-leather look of her hair, so that it assumes its more natural feminine cut, juxtaposing her sex with her attire. She is just as uncomfortable as he, Jake thinks. And they are playing a reluctant game of follow the leader.

After what seems like an eternity, Lulu slows the vessel to a crawl and turns back toward the shore before killing the engine. The rush of waves takes up the vacuum left by the cutting of the motor, but eventually even this dies away and the craft settles into the placid waters.

She was right, Jake thinks, looking back toward the city. It is an island.

Initially, no one moves, as though the next act were somehow unthinkable now that the moment has arrived. A final insult to the dead.

Lulu speaks, "Help me with this one, Jake." And as though someone throws a switch, Jake stands along with Bobby too and the three of them heave Israel over the edge. They wait quietly, looking into the gloom of the lake, but the body—wrapped and bound—does not float. Benji is next, with similar results.

The cool air coming off the lake catches in Jake's nostrils as he leans over the edge of the boat. It is a beautiful night, he thinks. And he allows his mind to wander back to Montreal, where he is a child again for just a moment, jogging in his father's footsteps down to the harbour where the tankers sound their horns and the world is slowly coming to life. Those were happier times.

But a sudden, blunt pain in the back of his neck pulls him away from the reverie too soon. He had not considered this. New Orleans fades on the horizon. So many mistakes.

Bobby is unaware of Lulu's plan until the paddle strikes the man's skull with a muted thwack. He wavers a moment, as though he might say something, then folds to the deck like a coil of rope. Bobby wants to protest, to beg in Jake's place, but she is too weak. Lulu's will glacial and constant.

"Take this," she says, tossing a sack in Bobby's direction as someone else might throw a dirty shirt. But Lulu is not unaware of her reticence, her burning desire to cradle the head of the man who saved her this evening. After all that had passed between them in the last year. The last two weeks.

"Do you really think he'll let us get away?" Lulu says. "That he'll let me go?"

Bobby is surprised by her astuteness at the same time that she is disheartened by her lack of observation. She is right, Bobby thinks. He will not let them get away with the money. But not because he wants it for himself. He is more likely to turn them all in, following his own confused morality. Only, Lulu is wrong about his attachment to her. It's over. She felt his yearning leave before she and Israel arrived at the house. He was empty then. Present only because he did not know where else to go.

But maybe Lulu does know this. Maybe that is why she has decided he is to die. Bobby bends without answering and slips the canvas sack over Jake's head.

Jake's skull is a nauseous thrum when he awakens, and he bites back the urge to vomit as his body is lifted. He is confused. The moon is gone and he can no longer feel the wind on his face.

"This is the last time," he hears. Lulu's voice. "I promise."

But no one answers. And then his body is swung like a pendulum, and he realizes he is wrapped in one of the coke sacks he dug from the cellar. His arms and legs are bound. The familiar sound of chain rings against the gunnels. They are going to drown him.

Jake's body hits the water with a slap, shoulders first. And afterward his feet. An awkward, lopsided toss. He screams, but too late. The noise is swallowed with his body. The lake bleeds into the sack almost immediately, filling the space around him—displacing the last chance for air—and he can feel himself sinking like an anchor. A sharp crackle in the water tells him that the boat is off, its propeller cutting a path back to shore. A moment later and the sound is gone. His eardrums burst under the pressure.

Initially, his heart slammed in the panic that accompanies death, but he is oddly calm as his sack becomes a bathysphere. Images surface and recede. His father fighting Jeffries. Adèle lonesome and staring at a deserted garden. The young girl sitting in the moonless kitchen. Lulu in the stairwell, waiting. Lulu in the dark. But it is the milk can that sticks with him, his first attempt in Montreal. And then habit takes over, the old nerve returning. Muscle memory. It is what he always wanted, after all. A chance to test himself.

This will be his greatest escape.

JOELE

Earlier in the day, not long after the murders, to which she is oblivious, Joele has discovered a package addressed to her at the counter of her hotel. It is large and hastily wrapped. She has to pay a boy to carry it upstairs to her rooms. A note is pinned to the package. She does not recognize the hand, but somehow she knows before reading that it is from Jake. It had been the sun through his window on Iberville that awakened her, bright as a dream. He was sleeping—a thorough slumber after days with nothing. She had been tempted to steal the envelope in his belt, but could not bring herself to do it. She can't understand why, even now. Perhaps it was the halo of light above his head. Perhaps not. She plucks the note. *Keep what you need*, it reads. *Rescue Bobby if she will be rescued. Perfect your own escape, but send the rest to the address below. We're all in need of saving sometime.*

The address is in Montreal and means nothing to her, but she is afraid to open the package and find what she suspects. Joele uses her own pocket knife to cut the string. You can never be too careful. Bobby learned this much from her, and perhaps she could learn more, given the chance. She is not, after all, far from that fierce, young girl Joele met years ago. Dark, frightened eyes the size of plates.

As Joele peels back the layers of brown paper and opens the box, her instincts are proven accurate yet again. She is conscious of the pulse in her neck. It is the sort of dream you have in childhood, complete with fairy godmothers.

She knows people who could fence the jewellery before nightfall. Even the bonds aren't an obstacle. And the cash, well, maybe she will deliver it herself, with Bobby. She has never been to Montreal. And then perhaps she will see Paris, the Left Bank. She is Creole, after all, and young. She has no other plans to keep her here, and life, above all else, is meant for living.

ACKNOWLEDGEMENTS

I would like to thank Todd Besant, Sharon Caseburg, Wayne Tefs, Kelly Stifura, Amber Robillard, Donna Sorfleet, Nancy Keech, Pat Sanders, and the long-suffering Caroline Bergeron for their help at various stages during the writing and editing of this book.

Some information about Harry Houdini and the era in which the novel is set was drawn from *Houdini on Magic* by the artist himself, *Montreal in Evolution* by Jean-Claude Marsan, *New Orleans Then and Now* by Lester Sullivan, *The American Variety Stage: Vaudeville and Popular Entertainment, 1870-1920*, from the Library of Congress, *The American Experience*, a PBS series, as well as numerous period newspapers and magazines.

The quote on pages 104-105 is from Alfred Lord Tennyson's "Ulysses." The epigraph is from Eli Mandel's poem "Houdini."